CW00410336

Deadly Season
A Carmedy & Garrett Mystery

By Alison E. Bruce

DEADLY SEASON:
A Carmedy & Garrett Mystery

This is a work of fiction. Names, characters, places and incidents either are the product of the author's imagination or are used fictitiously. And any resemblance to actual persons, living, dead (or in any other form), business establishments, events, or locales is entirely coincidental.

SECOND EDITION

August 2018

Published by Deadly Press
www.deadlypress.com

ISBN: 978-1-9994277-0-2

Cover designed by Deadly Press with photo by Marc-Olivier Jodoin on Unsplash

Dedication

This book is dedicated to: Sam, the barn cat who we thought was a Samantha; Nuptian the orphan kitten, rescued from the gutter; and Georgette, who saw my sister and me through four pregnancies and was a comfort through my sister's cancer and our family's grief.

Acknowledgements

I'd like to thank Nancy O'Neill who has been reading the good, the bad, and the ugly of my stories since… forever.

I'd also like to thank authors Melodie Campbell, Catherine Astolfo, Janet Bolin and Joan O'Callaghan for their feedback and support, Todd Barselow for being such a great editor, and Cheryl Kaye Tardif of Imajin Books, for introducing Kate Garrett to the world.

The City is somewhere in Canada.

The year is not now, but not far away.

1

December 16

Violent death was never pleasant. The cold hadn't diminished the smell of blood, piss and stools — or if it had, I didn't want to think about it.

A dart, the kind animal control officers use in their rifles, was sticking into the ribs. Instead of delivering a tranquillizer, its payload was poison. The feathery stabilizer at the end was red and green. Very seasonal.

"Do we know what know what the poison is, Chief?"

"Looks like cyanide. Samples were taken from the last victim. I'll let you know when the latest batch have been processed and compared."

Igor Thorsen, Chief of Detectives and my godfather, bent down and offered me his hand. I let him pull me out of the crouch I had been sustaining for several minutes while I examined the body.

I didn't need the help, but it was a

warm gesture on a cold night.

"I could use your help on this Kathleen," he said. "People are getting nervous but I can hardly free up a detective for a serial cat-killer. I can authorize support services for a week and the East Hills Neighbourhood Group will pay your fees."

I stripped off my gloves and ran my fingers through my hair, pushing back the auburn strands that had blown into my face. Time for a cut. Or maybe not. I didn't have to keep up the uniform code for keeping hair short or worn up.

I looked up at the Chief. Way up. And I'm not short. (Or particularly tall.)

I nodded.

My name is Kate Garrett. Up until recently, I had been a rookie detective in the violent crimes unit. The chief was my boss. Exactly one month ago my father, the Joe Garrett of Garrett Investigations, was killed in a pedestrian-vehicle incident. Now I was the Garrett of Carmedy and Garrett Investigations.

Last month I was a homicide detective. Now I was a pet P.I..

2

December 18

"Deck the halls with boughs of holly."

"I thought we agreed no holiday songs in the office."

"We agreed no holiday music in the office," I said, hanging fresh holly over the last window. "I didn't think that included me singing."

"Well it does," said Carmedy, scowling.

I gave him my best look of wounded sorrow.

He sighed.

I added my brave waif smile for effect. I took as many drama electives as I could fit in when doing my undergraduate degree in psychology and criminology. It's amazing how useful they proved to be in my professional life.

The cherry on top was a trembling lower lip a la Orphan Annie.

"Oh give it up," he said, laughing. "I

don't believe that quiver for an instant."

But I got you to laugh, I thought. These days, that's victory enough.

By the terms of my father's will, Carmedy and I became equal partners in his investigation agency. I took a leave of absence from the City Police Services to figure out what to do about that.

Carmedy thought I was crazy. Give up a secure job with benefits in this economy? But when had the economy not been an issue? I knew Dad didn't expect me to inherit so soon. Well, I didn't expect to lose my father so soon. Life happens.

He thought I was even crazier to take the cat-killer case. And he was pissed off I didn't consult him. Fair enough, but how did he expect me to say no to the Chief?

But that was yesterday's news. I was determined to reduce the tension between us.

For ten years we had been avoiding each other because of misunderstanding my darling father created.

I had miles to go in the grieving department, but was tired of being sad all the time and walking on eggshells around Carmedy was getting old.

"How are the reports going?"

"They're going." I glanced around the room and checked my handiwork. Not up to Thorsen standards but not too shabby either. "I'm making coffee. Want some?"

He looked at the half empty bottle of flat cola on his desk.

"I'll make you a café au lait."

"Yes, please."

I nodded, a bit distracted. Something was missing.

"I could help you finish the reports. I'm almost done the client statements."

Like hell budinski! It's took me days to make sense of and streamline his raw notes. I didn't say this though. I just shook my head.

"Then how about if I take your place on the patrol tonight?"

I laughed. "Miss prowling around in the cold and damp? No way! Besides, you're the one who told me if I took a job without consulting you, I'd have to do it myself."

I heard the sigh and turned around in time to see the eye roll.

"I get it," I said, hands up in surrender. "You have to work with Valerio on the Eldridge case. I want it tied up as tightly as possible too." Damn straight. That was my father's last case before he died.

He opened his mouth, but I didn't let him get a word out.

"There are year-end statements and month-end invoices on your plate as well. And, no doubt, you have plans for Christmas. Have I missed anything?"

He shook his head and managed a smile. I turned back to the office kitchenette. A few minutes later, I presented Carmedy with his café au lait.

"Don't worry Carmedy, I'll get the reports done in time for you to see I did it right. Now that I've cleared my head and have fresh coffee, I'm good to go. But first…"

I remembered what I forgot. There was one last paper bag to empty. I picked it up and climbed on top of my desk.

Carmedy yelped like a dog whose tail

had been stepped on. "What the hell?"

Pulling it out of the bag, I showed off a bunch of fresh mistletoe, wired into a ball and tied with a red ribbon. I stepped over my work to hang the ball between our desks.

The office had high ceilings so even from the desk I had to stretch on tippy-toes to secure the suction hook. I felt, rather than saw Carmedy move in, ready to catch me if I lost my balance.

When the job was done, I reached to use his shoulder to steady me before I jumped down. He did me one better and lifted me off the desk. We both looked up, but the mistletoe was out of range.

I think I was relieved. Carmedy looked disapproving, either because we didn't get to kiss or I put him in the position that we might. I went for the latter.

"Before you tell me it's unprofessional to have mistletoe in the office, the plant was originally hung to bring peace."

He went back to his desk muttering, "I knew that."

"I thought you might need

reminding."

3

The one thing that police work and private investigation have in common is reports. There were legal statements and client reports and, my new least favourite, the summaries we had to log with Police Services to keep our license to work with them.

Carmedy and Garrett Investigations was more than the incorporation of a couple of P.I.s. We were consulting detectives too... just like my childhood hero, Sherlock Holmes.

Not very like Sherlock Holmes though–especially now. Also, Chief Thorsen was no Inspector Lestrade. He was smarter and a lot harder to impress.

He had been one of my father's rookies. I'd known him all my life. That was one of the things that made my decision about whether or not to leave Police Services so hard.

Fortunately he gave me an exit that

allowed me to return. He let me combine compassionate leave with a training sabbatical. Sooner or later, though, I'd have to make a choice.

Because Thorsen trusted my father, his former partner and mentor, Garrett Investigations had preferential status. In theory, Carmedy & Garrett Investigations maintained that preferential status but I had to wonder, would Joe Garrett have taken a cat-killer case?

At four, Carmedy sat on the edge of my desk.

Carmedy was built along square lines, broad shouldered, deep chested, muscles designed for strength, not speed—the complete opposite of my father.

I used to think my father only hired him for muscle. I know better now, but when he wants to be, like now, Carmedy can be an immovable object.

I don't have my father's height or Carmedy's breadth, but I'm not easily intimidated or distracted. I kept working until I'd finished the section I was working on.

If he really wanted my attention, he could use my name. But that was another source of tension between us.

I was used to being referred to by my last name by my colleagues. Coming from a military background, Carmedy was used to the same. But for him, my father was Garrett. So, I called him Carmedy and he avoided using my name whenever possible. This time he used a shoulder tap to get my attention.

"Are you going home or upstairs before the stakeout?"

"Upstairs. I brought everything I'd need."

"Then you should go rest." He sounded like my mother. "If I tell you to go upstairs, will you take a quick nap, or will you go back to packing up your father's stuff?"

I shrugged. I almost rolled my eyes. I hate it when Carmedy reminds me of my mother. I love her dearly but I only need one of her in my life.

"Well?"

"I'll have a shower," I said, giving in.

"If I nap I might not want to get up again."

"Then go," he said, pointing to the inside door. "I'll call you in two hours if you haven't returned."

I nodded. This was an order I didn't mind following. Desk work was exhausting.

Flipping Carmedy a salute, I bypassed the inside steps and used the main entrance accessed from the fourth floor foyer – the location of my father's personal mailbox. Not much came by post anymore, but the odd sympathy card showed up from older relatives.

"Ms. Garrett!"

Great!

I slapped a smile on my face before turning to greet my new tenant.

When I inherited half my father's business, I also inherited a third interest in the building. Effectively, that meant I had control over the fourth floor where the office was and the attic where my father's flat was.

When the financial advisor from the third floor asked if the space across from the office was available for his son's new business, I figured it would be a good way of generating additional income.

Carmedy wasn't happy about it, but least he had the grace to say he wished I had consulted him, not that I should have done so.

Now I wondered if he knew something I didn't. Mother again.

"Good afternoon, Mr. Koehne." I took his outstretched hand.

"Always a pleasure to see you," he said, cupping my hand in both of his. "I was wondering if you had a chance to consider my offer."

I pulled away. "I already considered it, Mr. Koehne. I said no."

"Ms. Garrett . . . Kate . . . may I call you Kate?"

"I wish you wouldn't."

That put a small road bump in his pitch, but didn't slow him long enough for me to make my escape.

"The thing is, Outreach Dating has plenty of men on its lists, men who are looking for Ms. Right – or at least Ms. Right for now – but we don't have many women. I'll throw in a hair and face make-over before your interview. Not that you aren't lovely as is, but the fashion is for up-dos and swing-era-retro is in, so if you have an appropriate outfit…"

When I didn't respond, he added: "Wouldn't you like a date for New Year's Eve? All we have to do is book a time."

"Time is one thing I don't have. I'm also short on money. Specifically, I'm short the money you owe for last month's rent."

It was better than a boot in the rear for getting rid of the pest. He exited, with a hearty "Happy Holidays" before I had a chance to extract another promise he wouldn't keep.

Inside the apartment, I tried to avoid looking into the open living area. The bedroom was safe, cleared of emotional booby-traps.

My stepfather David helped me go through Dad's clothes, the bulk going to the Graveyard and Stinktown shanties where I knew they'd be distributed fairly. I only kept a few items–a Shetland cable-knit sweater Grandma Garrett made, Dad's academy issue sweats and t's, and his second best black trench coat. His best coat was buried with him.

The few personal items left out included a silver-backed brush set that had belonged to my great-grandfather and a few framed photos that were nostalgic but not sad. There were other things, packed away by David for me to look at later. I didn't ask. He didn't tell.

The living area was a whole other ball game.

Keep, store, give, and recycle bins were set up for sorting through the contents of the combination living room, dining room and kitchen. Everything had to be packed away so a contractor could come to replace the mouldy plaster ceiling.

"You couldn't have fixed it last spring, when the damp started," I said, looking heavenwards. "No. You had to leave it to me to deal with. I love you Dad, but you're a bum."

Sighing, I made a beeline to the fridge where a collection of leftovers waited.

Three-day old Punjabi, two-day old Greek and yesterday's pizza remains.

Making up a mixed plate of finger foods, I grabbed a beer with the plan of packing a book box or two while I ate.

Books were easy. Just pack them up for storage. Yes, there were a lot of them. My darling father loved electronic gadgets but he preferred to read hard copy books.

"Downloading information on a screen is convenient," he'd say. "Reading a book is a holiday. Rereading a good book is like visiting an old friend."

I guess he infected me with that outlook because I wouldn't dream of selling or, heaven forbid, recycling his library. Getting rid of his books would be like shooting his dog... or poisoning his cat.

"Why poison a cat in such an elaborate way?" I shook my head. "Doesn't make sense." I thought about that. "Does it have to?"

I dug through the bin I just packed and pulled out one of the books I remember him giving me to read when I was writing a paper on serial killers and mass murderers for high school sociology. It wasn't the most recent work even then, but Dad thought it was important enough to keep on his reference shelves. Tucking *The Anatomy of Motive* under my arm and grabbing my dinner, I left the packing to go eat and read in the bedroom.

A bugle tattoo woke me with a start. I'd have to change the ring tone on the landline before it gave me a heart attack. Apparently I fell asleep reading after my shower. I switched on and squinted blearily at Carmedy's face on the viewer. He gave a little cough and I noticed that my towel had slipped down.

4

In the detective's locker room, we all used the same space, regardless of gender or sexual orientation. There were a couple of cubicles for the extremely shy or religiously constrained, but otherwise the locker room was like an open concept dorm without the beds (although, the couch was comfortable to sleep on).

We were supposed to be like family. We looked out for each other, poked fun, offered a shoulder or a kick as needed but never behaved in a way that would be uncomfortable… at least, not on the job.

Evidently, my breasts made Carmedy uncomfortable, so I turned off the screen. That's when I noticed the time.

"Shit!"

"Do you want me to call Mrs. Parnell? I could push back your meeting half an hour."

I shook my head, forgetting he couldn't see now. "No need."

This wasn't the first time I had to go from zero to a hundred percent in a few minutes. I'd been doing it since high school.

Fifteen minutes later, Carmedy sent me off with a bag of sandwiches, fruit, and the keys to the company car. That put him way ahead of my mother. She'd never let me take her car.

East Hills was built around land reclaimed from the city dump. The landfill was turned into a park with trails winding over man-made hills, through formal and natural gardens and past two playgrounds. A wide avenue surrounded the park from which streets extended like bent spokes.

I knew the area well. My mother and David moved there a few years back, about the time the park was being developed.

Like most of the newer neighbourhoods, it contains mixed housing. Clumps of single family homes are broken up by groups of low-rise apartments. By provincial law there has to be thirty-percent tree cover in new development, but municipal regulations require clear lines of sight in public areas.

So, every house has a tree, but trees and hedges have to be spaced. The resulting effect is more like an architectural model than an organic neighbourhood.

You have to give a criminal credit for being able to work in that kind of setting. The inner-city neighbourhoods, who guarded their old growth trees, box hedges, and privacy, would have been an easier mark. Also, East Hills had a very active neighbourhood watch. Since the second time a dead cat had shown up on its owner's front steps, members had taken turns patrolling the area in pairs every night.

The one advantage a criminal had was that the patrol followed a strict routine. Handy for making sure none of the volunteers missed their time slot, it worked in the favour of anyone casing a house–or house cat.

The first change I made was to have the neighbourhood patrol mix things up.

Not everyone was happy with this.

"I'm missing *Senior Idol*," said Mrs. Parnell, checking her watch for the umpteenth time. "Paulo isn't going to be happy."

I'd only been half listening to Mrs. Parnell's running commentary on her neighbours. It was my second time out with the woman and most of the stories were reruns, but something didn't jibe.

"Isn't your husband's name Graydon?

"Of course, dear. Paulo's our neighbour. He watches *Senior Idol* with me–sometimes *World's Funniest Vids* too."

"Can't he come over later? You can stream them whenever you want."

She poked me in the arm. "Oh he doesn't come over dear. He watches through the window. I think he has limited access at home and I'm sure our wall screen has better resolution."

When Mr. "Just call me Gray like my hair" Parnell took his turn on patrol, I asked him about Paulo.

"Can't stand the little snot!" He stopped, took a deep breath, and let it out slowly. "Sorry. I'm sure he has reasons for being the way he is. I'm sure it's not his fault he's creepy."

"Creepy?"

"I shouldn't have said anything. Stella feels sorry for him. I suppose I do too." He started walking again. "That doesn't mean I have to like him."

"Of course not. What does he do that strikes you as creepy?"

Mr. Parnell looked heavenward, as if for guidance. "You'll think I'm crazy, but I think he has a thing for my wife."

Only professional training kept me from smiling.

"She thinks he's watching our vid. But I caught him watching her. I don't think she's the only one either."

That was nothing to smile about.

At one, the last patrol called it a night. In the course of the evening I had walked or driven around with five members of the watch and covered most of the area. No one segment could be watched all evening, but the apparent randomness of the schedule would make it hard for the cat-killer to act.

After one, everyone who was going to be home tonight would be home with their cats in and alarms set. Even so, I hung around for a little longer.

I sat in the company's beat-up hybrid and sipped on the coffee David made me. Carmedy's coffee was so terrible I stopped by my mother and David's house and begged a refill of my thermos.

While I was there, I asked David if he knew about the suspected peeping tom. He didn't, but he offered to ask around. David was the kind of man women liked talking to, an occupational hazard when you're a doctor and psychotherapist.

Paulo Crabbe definitely warranted further investigation. A background check revealed that he worked at a paper recycling plant. A quick search confirmed that cyanide compounds were used in processing paper.

Of course, cyanide had so many industrial and household uses getting hold of it wasn't a challenge. Still, he was the best lead I'd got.

Besides patrolling with the watch, I'd scanned police incident reports for complaints.

There were the families that had been reported for not sorting their garbage properly and a couple who thought their dog was entitled to poop wherever it wanted had several complaints and an outstanding fine against them.

And there were the dozen or so petty grievances that one neighbour has against another, even in a friendly community, going back over the last two years.

None involved animal cruelty, domestic abuse or arson.

No cat-killers jumped out of the crowd.

Hungry, I reached for my dinner bag.

Give him his due, Carmedy put together a good sandwich. Not as good as David's Reuben but way better than ham and processed cheese sandwiches my mother put in my lunch before she decided I was old enough to make my own.

Half a sandwich later, I moved to a new spot with a view of the park. Someone was taking a walk. Doing up my coat, I decided to see who was out so late.

As soon as I stepped away from the car I activated the recorder on my eCom. In a low voice I told it where I was going and why.

An app would add the time and GPS coordinates to my report and a code word from me would download the information with a request for help to Emergency Response Coordination.

We hadn't had a major snowfall yet. The paths were clear and grass was visible through the light powder. I plotted an intercept course across the lawn, walking purposefully but not rushing.

As I walked, I sent out a ping to make sure this wasn't a member of the watch. It was the same ap that people had been using since the turn of the century to tell them when their friends were close by.

Not a member of the watch.

I took a couple of photos. Even with enhancement, they were probably too far away.

While I kept my eye on my quarry — who was probably some innocent guy out for a stroll—I tried to work out height, weight and gender, even the colour of his coat. I should have been looking where I was stepping.

My heel set down in something soft and slid forward. I tried to catch myself but ended up landing hard on my tail bone.

"Fu–" Then the smell hit me. "Crap!"

5

I'd landed in dog shit. In my pocket my eCom alarm went off. My quarry was now running away.

"What is the nature of your emergency?" asked the ERC operator.

"False alarm," I said.

"You really have to come up with a better emergency word Garrett."

"I thought I had."

When I got back to the car, a blue and white was waiting. It looked pretty sleek beside the company clunker.

"What's up Garrett? You stink."

Just my luck, it was Zander Mohr. He was one of my father's old cronies. He was also my field training officer when I was hired. He saw it as his duty to keep me humble.

"Hold on a sec."

I wrenched opened the passenger side door of Dad's car and grabbed a handful of napkins from the glove compartment.

Heading for the nearest receptacle, I wiped the worst of the mess off as I walked. When I got back, Mohr was holding out an industrial sized wet-wipe.

"Thanks."

"So?'

"I was checking on someone in the park and slipped on dog poo."

"I can smell that. What happened to the other guy?"

"Got spooked and ran away."

"Natural response to an alarm going off. I heard it from the other side of the park."

I winced. "Too loud?"

"Nope," said Mohr, shaking his head. "Just loud enough. Go home, Garrett. Or go to a laundry. Get outta here. The cats are safe tonight."

It was three by the time I got back to the loft. I'd been staying there more often than not, what with all the packing I needed to do. Not tonight, though. Tonight I'd go straight to bed with a nice cup of tea.

I didn't bother turning on lights.

There was enough ambient light streaming through the front windows to navigate.

The light in the bedroom was filtered by a large stained glass panel set into the dividing wall.

Whether I stayed or rented the apartment, that panel was mine. I helped design it and I cajoled Mum and David, the Thorsens and a bunch of Dad's friends, including Mohr, to pitch in so I could get it made as an office warming gift.

I was young and foolish and though a thumbprint and a magnifying glass was the perfect image for a consulting detective.

Diplomatic as usual, Dad announced it was exactly what he needed for his apartment.

After a quick shower to get rid of any residual stink, I headed for the kitchen and turned on the bar lights.

Once the kettle was on, I pulled up a stool and started looking through some of the odds and ends I found while boxing books.

My father was highly organized in the office, probably thanks to Carmedy. At home he had a habit of shoving things on top of books on the shelf.

I'd found old birthday cards, junk mail and a number of recycled mailers that Dad used to store paperwork.

I picked up one of the mailers. It was thick and heavy. The postmark indicated it was twelve years old.

The kettle started singing its shrill note. I made a pot of tea and returned to the mailer. Might as well take a look while the tea steeped.

An old-style memory card slid out of the envelope with a neatly bound file folder.

I felt a shiver of anticipation rippled down my neck, making my shoulders twitch. The card was the kind my father used in his audio recorder. In addition to official recordings and reports, he found it useful to keep a more conversational record of his thoughts on a case.

I set aside the plastic-cased card for later. Instead, I thumbed through the report copies and yellowed newspaper clippings, trying to get a sense of what the case was about and why my father would keep the file.

One headline on one tear sheet answered my questions: "Local detective shot defending domestic abuse victim."

This was my father's last case as a police officer.

6

December 19

Bleary-eyed, I shuffled into the office at nine.

Carmedy looked up from his mail. "How did it go last night?"

I grunted and automatically went to the kitchenette to start the coffee. It was already made.

"I figured you'd be down soon, so I started a pot. I also brought bagels and cream cheese to go with the peach compote."

I gazed at him for an uncomprehending minute, then at the counter which held a bag of bagels, a tub of cream cheese and six mason jars of peach preserves, one of which was half empty.

I turned back to Carmedy, hoping for enlightenment.

"Mr. Koehne's sister has a small

business producing peach preserves," he explained. "Peach jam, peach syrup, peach chutney—you get the idea. He's marketing the stuff for her. He has a display set up on his front counter."

I poured coffee and made up a bagel with cream cheese and jam, licking the knife when I was done. "This is good!"

"That's why I got six jars," he said, grinning. "And why one of the jars is half empty. Oh, and Koehne asked me to deliver an envelope to you. It's on your desk."

I set my breakfast on the desk and opened the envelope. It was the rent cheque.

"Did you lean on him?" she asked.

He pretended not to hear the question.

"Carmedy?"

He responded without looking up. "Maybe a little."

I nodded. Putting the cheque to one side, I sat and took a sip of coffee.

"Carmedy."

This time he met my gaze. "Yes."

"Never, ever make coffee again." I

tried to stay serious despite the comical look of surprise on his face. "I don't blame you. My father couldn't brew a decent cup of coffee either."

I pushed my mug away and picked up the cheque again. "About this, thanks."

"No digs about being able to handle it yourself?"

I shook my head. "I don't want to handle Koehne at all. I was an idiot to rush into renting the space."

Carmedy said nothing but his eyes were so wide with shock, I started to laugh.

"I must be tired if I said that aloud."

That made him laugh. Two laughs in two days. I was on a roll.

While I prepared the coffee, Carmedy managed to surprise me.

"Tell me about your case."

"The cat-killer case?"

Dumb question, I know, but he caught me off-guard. He didn't get snarky about it. He just waited for me to get over it and start talking.

I started with the usual avenues and

how they hadn't produced any likely suspects. No relevant criminal activity. No lead on where the poison or darts was procured.

"Although there is one interesting thing," I said. "The darts weren't preloads that were tampered with. They're hand loaded, the kind that wildlife rangers use so they can customize the dosage for the animal and length of time they need the target down."

I'd spent a couple of hours researching the topic and finding out how easy it was to order the necessary equipment to make custom darts. On the other hand, you can't just buy a tranquilizer pistol or rifle through legitimate channels without a permit. Not in Canada.

Fortunately, as a police officer, I didn't have that problem. I didn't mention this to Carmedy. He might worry about me using him for target practice. Instead I skipped to the poison.

"There's no point trying to track down the source of the cyanide until I get the lab's profile."

Carmedy nodded. "I agree. Too many potential sources. So, meanwhile you beat the pavement."

"Basically. By talking to the watch, I've come up with a few persons of interest."

I told him about Paulo Crabbe, the suspected peeping tom.

"Then there's Mr. Theo Konstantin. According to most of the watch, he just doesn't like new people. Mrs. Parnell thinks he's a bit sinister, but that might be because he reminds her of Nosferatu — which is a bit harsh."

"Mrs. Parnell says I have the voice of Hugh Jackman playing Wolverine."

I thought about it and nodded. Mrs. Parnell had a point. Of course, Mrs. Parnell thought that Paulo Crabbe looked a bit like the guy in the Nabob ads. She didn't specify which storyline so I couldn't picture him.

"Anyway, I asked who had changed their habits since I joined the watch patrols."

"And?"

I closed my eyes to view my mental white board of notes. "Marc and Evelyn Chauvelin used to walk their cat nightly, but not since the changes. Mr. Parnell says it's because they can't coordinate with the patrol anymore.

"Mrs. Djohns stopped going out, but since she's ninety three, it might just be the cold. Then there's Ms. Cole. She's more elusive than Mr. Konstantin. I get the impression she's agoraphobic. She won't go out at night if there's anyone strange in the neighbourhood and she won't go out in the daytime at all.

"Then there's Crabbe, of course. He's hasn't been seen out and about much lately which lends credence to him being a peeping tom if nothing else."

"You think he's good suspect?"

I shrugged. "I'll interview him this afternoon. If I have time, I'll drop in on the Chauvelins as well. And don't worry. I'll finish the last report before I go."

Carmedy said nothing but went to check the pot for more coffee. He brought it back and topped up my cup.

"Actually, I did the last report this

morning."

I stared at him.

"You'll need to prepare it for publication," he said. "I didn't want to mess with your system, but it occurred to me that doing the report on your father's last case might–"

"Might be too emotional for me?"

It was difficult but I would have finished it today.

"Nah."

He put a little extra gruff into his tone.

"You're tough as nails. But it might seem inappropriate for a daughter to report on her father's work. It might seem biased."

That was the worst excuse I ever heard, but I nodded as if it was perfectly logical. Silently I thanked the mistletoe for its salubrious effect.

"So, if it wasn't the reports. What kept you up all night?" he asked.

Oh good god! He was going to mother me again.

7

"Have you been up all night going through Joe's stuff? You should get some help with that so you don't dwell on it so much."

I wanted to snap at him. It was my job. I was his daughter and executor of his estate. Magnus would round up a posse when it was time to move things, but it was my job to sort through the remains of my father's life.

Carmedy shook his head.

"I'd order you back to bed if I thought it would work."

"Order?" I forced my tired eyebrows to rise.

He grinned.

"I am the senior partner. And you're the one who put my name above yours on the door."

I looked at the mistletoe. Peace. It would be a lot easier to maintain if we collaborated instead of butting heads.

I took my coffee to the couch. This was where my father seated clients when he wanted to make them feel comfortable. I curled up at one end of the three-seater. Carmedy sat at the other end.

I confessed.

"I was going through one of Dad's case files. I knew that his last police case involved domestic violence. I remember reading the papers at the time. There were conflicting reports of the incident depending, I suppose, on who provided the information to which reporter. I tried to sort it out while we waited for my father to come out of surgery. I figured I'd come up with a theory and Dad would tell me if I was right or not."

"Assuming he knew. Trauma often causes the victim to block out events immediately before, during and after the event."

Sometimes I forgot that Carmedy was a combat veteran and had been through his own medical and emotional trauma.

"You're right. Like my father said after the surgery, we constantly train for the moment we hope will never come, when we need to act without thinking about it. And a good job too."

"He said all that after surgery?"

I smiled.

"I didn't say how long after surgery."

Carmedy smiled back. I wondered if I could get the florist to source me fresh mistletoe year round.

"What theory did you put together?"

I sat up a little straighter.

"I'm not sure if I remember my rational, but I deduced that the news reports were all partly correct and fundamentally wrong.

"One report had the shot being aimed at my father, and he dodged getting killed. Two other reports insisted that my father threw himself in front of the shooter to protect either the abused wife or the other detective on the scene.

"All agreed that my father got off three shots and that at least one hit the husband. Since they all agreed, I took that to be a potentially fact-based statement, not just hearsay."

"What did the other witnesses say?"

"Nothing."

Carmedy leaned in. "Nothing?"

I nodded.

"The only witnesses to the shooting were Mr. and Mrs. Collins and my father's partner, a rookie who resigned after the incident. Mrs. Collins was unresponsive. Or as one reporter put it..."

I made air quotes with the hand that wasn't holding my coffee. "A victim of abuse for years, the poor woman was unable to respond to any of the questions put forth by this reporter."

"You memorized the line?"

I shrugged. "It wasn't hard. It was quoted over and over in other articles. She never made a statement to the police either. She checked herself into the Mental Health Centre. But I found that out later.

"At the time, the big news was that, in the ensuing confusion, the husband got away. A blood trail indicated he was wounded. Police were in hot pursuit. That's the last I ever heard."

"At the time," said Carmedy.

"At the time."

I hugged my coffee cup for warmth. It

was empty but still warm and I was feeling chilled, a sure sign I hadn't got enough sleep. Maybe I should let Carmedy order me up to bed after all. Maybe I'd let him tuck me in...

Back up, Garrett. He's off limits. I continued my debriefing.

"I couldn't quite face listening to my father's recorded notes, but he saved articles and news bytes from the aftermath. I ran a search through public and police data bases for more information. Blake Collins, the man who shot my father, was never found. He dropped off the grid and has managed to stay off it ever since."

"That's highly suspect. What does it have to do with our case?"

I tilted my head to one side.

"Our case, Kemosabe?"

His face scrunched up like he'd just sucked a lemon. I let him off the hook and continued.

"There are two intersection points. One, it happened in East Hills. Two, a neighbour reported that Collins had been back to the house. He took a couple of suitcases, the car and his wife's cat, which he apparently hated and threatened to strangle."

"So, after all this time, you think he's returned to threaten other cats?"

When he said it like that, it did seem a bit unlikely.

"I know it's a bit tenuous. I looked for more information in police records. Mrs. Collins moved and seems to have changed her name. Even so, East Hills is the logical place for Collins to return. If he returned."

Now my argument seemed weak to my ears.

"Never mind," I said, putting down my cup. "It's just a weird coincidence."

"Probably it's a coincidence" said Carmedy. "Maybe it's not. We'll keep it in mind."

I grimaced.

"No, I'm not trying to humour you," he said, getting up and pulling my legs into the space he had been sitting.

I took the hint and lay down. In what seemed to me like a blink of an eye, he was putting a blanket over me. I was going to get tucked in after all. Too bad I was too sleepy to appreciate it.

"Sleep on it." He tucked the blanket under my feet. "Weird shit happens all the time and this case has been weird from the get-go."

8

I woke up alone.

Carmedy left a message saying that he was meeting with Valerio. I was betting it would include lunch and felt a bit envious. They were probably eating a gourmet, locally sourced lunch while I was going to have bagels, cream cheese and peach jam.

Okay, maybe I wasn't that envious.

I finished processing the report and started proofreading. Honestly, I doubted anyone had time to read this stuff. If they did, they'd find everything properly referenced and interlinked to corresponding digital documents. No auditor would complain my i's and t's weren't dotted and crossed.

Still, a girl could only take so much admin crap before having a meltdown.

So, I logged out and got out of the office before Carmedy came back to ask if I was done yet. Since I had laundry to do, I went home.

I didn't keep track of Magnus' shifts, so I had no business being disappointed he wasn't home. It's not like I'd been around much either. Still, I was disappointed. Magnus and I were much better friends now that we weren't together as a couple. We had practice living together from when we were both students and we had a history.

I didn't have to explain how shitty my job could be. He didn't need to explain how sad his could be working as a pediatric nurse. At the same time, we appreciated the humour that came our way too and shared it without fear of being labelled crude, crass or ghoulish.

When I started thinking that way, moving into my dad's place seemed wrong. Then he'd bring a party home and having my own space seemed like a great idea. Until I had to do laundry.

Screw it! I didn't have to make a decision yet. That settled... or not settled for now, I was able to attack a few chores like taking out the recycling, watering my poor forsaken plants and cleaning out my closet. All mostly mindless tasks that helped me think. Give me enough closets and I could solve the problems of the world.

Cats.

When I took the case, I concentrated on the pet owners. Leaving a dead animal on a door step is a pretty personal message. Thinking that the cat-killer had an issue with the families seemed reasonable. That didn't make it correct, especially since I couldn't find a common denominator between the families other than cat ownership.

If Paulo Crabbe was the killer, it might be his way of getting attention, or a step toward killing the women he watched. It wouldn't be personal so much as staged for effect.

If Blake Collins was the cat-killer, it might be personal, but directed against his wife. If that was the case, maybe she had returned to the neighbourhood too. Or it might be directed against the neighbours who called the police. I should get the details and follow that up.

If it was someone else... Nah. There

was no point going there until I'd eliminated the suspects I had.

All my clothes were out of the closet and arranged in piles on my bed.

I could bag up the stuff I was getting rid of and organize the rest. Or I could hang up the stuff that needed hanging and the use rest of my time, and my police login, to get the names of the Collins' neighbours. I opted for the latter.

At five, Carmedy called.

"Are you coming back tonight?"

I looked at my bed and nodded. "I'll be back after I'm finished in East Hills."

"Are you still tired? I could go if you want."

"I'm good."

Wild horses couldn't keep me away. I'd just found out that Mrs. Parnell used to live beside Mr. And Mrs. Collins.

9

Mrs. Parnell begged off, claiming her back was acting up.

"She's in the middle of watching a documentary series on reality shows," her husband explained. "She convinced the channel is going succumb to pressure from its sponsors and pull it from the Net."

"Is that likely?"

He shrugged. "Who knows? Who cares? I'm happy to get out of the house."

"And I'm happy to have your company," I said, though I was also disappointed about missing a chance to pick Mrs. Parnell's memory. She was Miss Morrow when she lived in the apartment next to the Collins. They weren't as old a married couple as they seemed. Or were they?

"How long have you and your wife been together?"

"We've been married seven years."

He gave a little cough.

"But we've been together for more than ten."

Only years of training kept me from showing how happy I was.

"Then you were together when she lived in the geared-to-income townhouses."

We weren't walking very swiftly to start with. Now he slowed to a snail's pace.

"How do you know about that?"

"I've been working my way back, looking at criminal activity in the neighbourhood."

He nodded and picked up the pace.

"You mean what happened to poor Irene."

"Irene Collins, yes. I was hoping your wife might be able to fill in some gaps. Maybe you can instead."

Another hesitation.

"I didn't live with her back then. I just stayed over a couple of nights a week when my wife was away."

"Oh. I didn't mean to pry…"

Of course I did. That's was my job.

However, there are ways and ways of prying. One of them is to shut up and let the other person fill the awkward silence.

It didn't take long.

"It's no biggy." He flexed his shoulders as if shrugging off something unpleasant. "My ex-wife and I had an open marriage. I just realized too late that I was made to be monogamous. I might complain about her, but Stella is the love of my life."

He cleared his throat noisily.

"You won't tell her I said that, will you?"

"I won't say a word if you tell me what you know about the Collins."

He didn't know much. I shared my carafe of coffee with him and even a couple of Magnus's homemade cookies, only to find out that most of what he knew was hearsay.

Stella said Collins yelled at his wife all the time. There had been noise complaints. Then there was the shooting. He had disappeared before he could be arrested. All things I knew.

"I only talked to Irene a couple of

times about the weather or the latest municipal cutback. Time-of-day stuff. Even so, she struck me as a pleasant and intelligent young woman. Smarter than her husband, who talked more and said less. It was a real shame what happened to her…"

Finally. Something useful.

"What happened to her?" I did my best not to sound too excited.

"Well, she closed down completely, didn't she?" Gray shook his head. "We thought that she might be able to make a fresh start, especially after her father helped her buy the house. We even tried to befriend her after we bought a house and got married. After all, we're still neighbours."

"You are?"

"Didn't Stella mention her?" He scratched his head. "Didn't I? Anyway, she goes by Irene Cole now. She lives on the other side of Crabbe. Fortunately for her, there's the access lane to the park between them. He can't spy on her the way he does on my wife."

He grunted. "Creep."

10

December 20

The phone woke me up at eight. It was Magnus. At least, he said he was Magnus. He sounded so gruff, it could have been his twin brother, a fellow detective, Xavier. (Their parents were classic X-Men fans.)

"Is there something you were meaning to tell me?"

"Huh?"

"If you're going to pull a midnight run, you need to finish packing before I get home from work."

"Huh?" I needed coffee or, better still, more sleep. "What the hell are you talking about Magnus?"

"Your suitcase is gone. Your clothes are in bags or piles ready to bag or box."

Now that I was seeing the light, I decided that coffee was the way to go. I put on a hands-free and headed for the kitchen.

"I was cleaning out, not clearing out. The bag, singular, is stuff I'm getting rid of and you still have my suitcase since you borrowed it for that cruise last spring. As for the rest, I ran out of time and didn't get a chance to put stuff back."

"You got distracted."

Some days that man knew me too well. Since I didn't feel the need to tell him he was right, silence hung between us until Magnus broke it. When he did, he sounded like the gentler twin I knew and loved.

"You haven't made a decision yet, have you?"

"No. Do you want me to go?"

His sudden snort of laughter made me lose track of my coffee scoop count. I had to start over.

"No way! This decision is yours to make not mine."

"But it's your apartment," I whined.

Again there was silence, then a sigh I could almost feel.

"I just got in and I need a shower and my tea. I told you when you moved in you could stay as long as you needed. It's up to you to figure out what you need now."

He disconnected and I cursed him for being so reasonable.

Dumping the beans back into the canister, I started over. The familiar ritual of making coffee, showering and putting together leftovers to have for breakfast gave me time to think. Since I wasn't ready to think about where I was going to live, I thought about Irene Collins/Cole.

I needed to talk to her, but that wasn't going to be easy if she was as reclusive as I'd been told. It would be better to arm myself with more information. Right now I didn't have enough reason to invade her space. It was a longshot that her husband was involved in the cat killings and I couldn't very well tell her I wanted to know what happened because of my father.

Or could I?

The answer to that question might be in my father's personal logs. I wasn't sure I was ready to listen to them.

I pulled out the memory card and refilled my coffee cup. I took a sip of black courage and plugged the card into an adaptor for my eCom.

"Damn! Is this thing working finally?"

Dad sounded tired and irritated. Those were the days when he used to come to me for tech support. He complained that electronics were getting to be like child-proof medicine bottles. Only the kids could work them.

"To briefly recap the notes I lost when this damn device ate them, I have a problem with my new detective. She's intelligent and compassionate and going to get herself into trouble if she doesn't learn to step back. Taking a case too personally doesn't help anyone and can put people in danger. I almost hit her today, for example."

There was a rumbling chuckle that I remembered well. Dad was laughing off his bad mood. It was a trick he taught me. Laughter can trick your body into thinking you don't really want to cry, kill someone or just give up. It cleared the mind.

There was a rustle of paper. He was consulting his case notes.

"Okay. There were three callouts to the Collins' home before the case was sent to the

bullpen. None of them screamed spousal abuse but Mohr had a feeling and went to the chief with it. Mohr would make a decent detective if you could pry him out of community policing.

"During our initial interviews, it was seemed to me that Collins was verbally abusing his wife. At the very least, he showed no real respect for her. Marten says that Mrs. Collins showed her bruises on her upper arms. She thinks there's more but Mrs. Collins refuses to be examined. Marten has a certain prejudice in this area, but her interview seems…"

There was a thump, accompanied by a faint cry.

"Damn!"

There were sounds of movement, then nothing. The recorder had been turned off.

Then there was faint music in the background. Beethoven's Pastoral. Or, as I always thought of it, thanks to Disney's Fantasia, the centaur music. That probably meant that I had woken up from a bad dream. Mum must have been at her night class, because it was only when she was out that I could get away with tucking up on the couch in front of the plasma screen. Otherwise, I had to be satisfied with my tablet in bed.

"Forget the details."

My father's voice was pitched lower than before.

"Let's get to the stuff I couldn't write up in the report.

"In absence of a psychiatric evaluation, I'm going to go out on a limb and say that Collins is a high functioning sociopath.

"Since he's also handsome and capable of being charming, he can fool most of the people most of the time… until he wants something, that is. Then he becomes manipulative and abusive.

"I saw it when it was clear Marten and I weren't going away until we had completed our interviews. He tried to cajole, then coerce me into letting him join his wife.

"He argued that his wife was phobic. When I asked what she was afraid of, he laughed and said 'Everything.' When I asked if she had sought professional help, he said 'No way! I don't trust those mind-fuckers.'"

There was a pause. In the background I could hear the thunder that accompanied the music when the centaurs were finding shelter from the storm.

"I can't say I entirely trust psychologists either. Or maybe I just don't trust the one my wife keeps staying out with after class."

He was talking about David. I knew that my mother was seeing him back then, which is one of the reasons I kept having nightmares. She said it was just coffee and intelligent conversation, but I was too much my father's daughter not to see the signs.

I didn't know my father knew. I guess I just hoped he didn't.

I turned off the recorder. I was going to get bogged down in my own bad memories if I continued this way. Instead, I ran the file through my voice to speech transcriber. While it processed, I took my coffee to the bathroom so I could shower and get ready for the day.

The morning went smoothly. Koehne avoided me in the lobby. Carmedy didn't say anything about me leaving early and he let me make the coffee. This partnership might work after all.

I wrote up my case notes in hope that

something about the cat-killer would pounce out at me. The trouble was, all the activity at night was keeping the cats safe, but all the killer had to do was lay low until we went away.

Even the most enthusiastic member of the East Hills group couldn't keep up this level of watchfulness forever.

"I was just thinking that we might be creating too much of a presence in the neighbourhood."

Carmedy looked at me blankly.

"Sorry, thinking aloud," I said.

"You're suggesting we should make it look like we've given up–draw the cat-killer into the open?"

We? Now it's we? I didn't voice the question. I'd take his help if he was offering.

"Yeah. We need to narrow the field."

I reminded him about the changes I'd made in how the neighbourhood patrol worked.

"If they went back to the original routine, maybe we could lull the perp into a false sense of security."

I hated the word perp, but otherwise

agreed.

"That's what I'm thinking. But I think we need to close off the park."

"Close off the park?" he asked, eyebrows furrowed.

I smiled and nodded.

"Consider, since no suspicious vehicles appear in correspondence to the killings, we can assume the cat-killer lives in the neighbourhood and hunts on foot. If we cut off access to the park the shortcut to everywhere, we might limit his or her territory."

"Assuming we could close the park, we'd have to let him strike again to narrow the field."

That was true. I had to think about this some more and I would do that best without Carmedy staring at me. I kept wondering what he was thinking.

"We need lunch," I announced. "I'm feeling the need for pizza. You go for pizza and I'll see what I can do about the park."

Carmedy looked at me strangely. "Shit."

"What?" I asked.

"For a moment, you sounded just like Joe."

11

"Coffee," I announced to the empty room. "I need more coffee."

What I really needed was time to gather my thoughts. The ritual of cleaning the machine, measuring the beans and water, then washing the cups as the coffee brewed gave me that.

What did Carmedy mean when he said I sounded like my father? At least he didn't say I looked like my father. Not that my father wasn't a good looking man, and I'm not just saying that because I'm his daughter, but he wouldn't have made an attractive woman.

I think I'm attractive. I'm pretty sure Carmedy thinks so too. Though sometimes it's hard to tell.

I'm generally good at reading people but...

I switched tracks.

What if the cat-killer used a microchip reader? It was a commonly available piece of technology.

All the cat victims had good homes and carried electronic tags, as per animal control bylaws. Maybe returning the animals was a strange form of kindness, not an attack.

What if it was all about the cats?

If I was going to ask Thorsen to close the park, I'd need more than a couple of what ifs.

An hour later, Carmedy handed me a piece of pizza and watched me take the first bite. I didn't know why he worried. The man might be a jerk sometimes, but he knew how to order pizza. Today he got four-cheese, antipasto with pesto sauce. One bite and I felt like I was in heaven, or a really good pizzeria.

"Mm."

I felt a dribble of sauce on my chin. Carmedy handed me a napkin then looked at my monitor and frowned.

"Proofed the annual report?" he asked.

"Half done. Then the words started swimming."

"Close the park?"

"Not yet. I was following up on a few ideas about the cat-killer while you were gone."

I pushed back my chair so I didn't have to crick my neck to make eye contact. "I don't think the pet owners are relevant, only the cats. My guess is that there are more dead cats that didn't have tags to identify their homes."

"And you've corroborated this how?"

"I talked to the Humane Society. Obviously they don't get queries from owners who don't tag their animals, but they do get complaints about strays. Not in East Hills, though. None at all. Not for months."

I took another bite of pizza and let Carmedy cogitate while I masticated. Then I continued.

"It isn't proof, but it is suggestive. If we look for a dumping ground, or fresh burial locations, we might be able to narrow our focus. I also looked into getting the services of a cadaver dog. It would make the job easier, but I'm not sure the neighbourhood will spring for the expenses."

"Fine, I'll follow up on it this evening."

"We both can."

Help I could use, but I wasn't going to have him take over my case.

"I'd rather you finish the proofing. I want to have time to go over them a last time before I go home for the holidays."

Dropping the pizza onto my desk, I forced myself to swallow, not spit my last bite.

Did he think I was incapable? Did he think at all before he spoke?

I pushed aside the pizza and my notes, called up the report and turned away from him, and repositioned my chair.

"I'll have it done soon."

He was at my shoulder, probably at parade rest. Once a soldier always a soldier. Well, I was a cop, and I knew at least as well as he did how to check a damned report.

An incoming call forced him to go to his own desk.

"Hey, Chief."

"Hello, Jacob. Is Kathleen with you?"

He pushed a button and Thorsen's face appeared on my screen.

I forced a smile I didn't feel. "I'm here, Chief. What can I do?"

"This isn't business," Thorsen said. "I'm out shopping for gifts and I want to know if your mother is currently on a diet. I want to get her some handmade chocolates but…"

I laughed, suddenly feeling much better.

"Mum's not dieting."

"Well, it's not like she needs to, but…"

"I know what you mean. She tries out every new diet anyway but not over the holidays. Or maybe she goes on a turkey and blintz diet. Who knows?"

Thorsen gave a bark of laughter cheering me up even more.

"One other thing, Maggie made me promise that I'd remind you that tomorrow night we celebrate the Yule. You and Jacob are expected at the house by six o'clock."

My smile faded.

"I can't. I have a cat-killer to catch. The felines of East Hills are depending on me."

"I'll take the stakeout," Carmedy said. "You go to dinner."

Thorsen heaved a sigh so heavy, I half expected the flimsies on my desk to ruffle.

"I'll assign an extra patrol car to the area," Thorsen said. "Both of you are expected tomorrow night. No excuses. Maggie is counting on you. The girls are counting on you. And I will send out a posse to detain and deliver you if need be."

I sighed and papers did ruffle.

"Don't disappoint me, Kathleen. This time, of all times, we need to be together. Getting through the holiday will be hard enough as it is."

"Oh shit. Of course," Carmedy muttered.

"I won't disappoint you," I said.

"I know you won't."

"Look Chief, can I ask a small favour while I have you? It might help if we could close the park in the evening for a few nights. Who should I suck up to?"

"I'll get the patrol to put up some

signs tonight. You better talk to the East Hills group too."

"Thanks Chief."

I cut the connection but continued to stare at the blank screen. "Oh shit," was right. Ever since my father started inviting his new partner to the Thorsen gathering, I only went over for Yuletide if Carmedy was out of town.

As if his ears were burning from my thoughts, Carmedy cleared his throat the way a kid might if getting the attention of a feared teacher.

"You know, there's no reason I can't start going over the sections of the report you've finished."

I nodded. With a few keystrokes, I sent the document to his terminal.

Carmedy cleared his throat again, using the same cautious tone.

"We haven't got a lot of time to wrap up the case of the cat-killer. Thorsen offering a patrol car made me think, if we made the perp think the police were taking over and that they were limiting themselves to the park, we might be able to set a trap."

I looked over at him, brows furrowed. It sounded good, so why was he talking like I might bark at him?

"That means, you'd have to follow up on the leads you have between now and tomorrow evening. After that, we have to look like we're stepping back."

"Okay."

What the hell did he expect me to say?

"You are the one who got us into this case in the first place." He glanced over the report on the screen. "I see you've done all the setup..." He did a double take. "This is really well organized." "Surprised?"

He winced. "Why don't I finish this up? The rest of the proofing too. Then you can concentrate on the East Hills case."

I swear he was holding his breath. I didn't get it. Then I did. I guess I had been a bit touchy. I wasn't the only one walking on eggshells these days.

"Okay. But I'll still need to format the parts you add."

Carmedy let out his held breath and I tried not to grin.

An hour later, Carmedy was finished. He was either more efficient or less fussy about proofing than I was. Falling back into his sergeant major mode, he asked me for an update.

I waved him over to my desk where I was working on a map of the neighbourhood. "The red x's mark houses where dead cats showed up. The green o's mark the most likely suspects. I added a few after my talk with the Humane Society. As you can see, the red x's are spread out but are never far very from the park. The o's fall in two clumps."

"What are the shaded areas?"

"Places where digging has been done in the three months. If any of the sites had been used for cat burials, the workers would probably have found evidence. I'm also running lifetime background checks on the suspects. If they were sixteen or over and got a parking ticket, I'll know."

"Who have you talked into doing that?"

I bumped his shoulder with mine.

"Still a cop, Carmedy. Still have access."

At three, Carmedy announced that he was going to take a nap. He was going out with the patrol so I could canvas my suspect pool.

"Want to use Dad's place?" I asked.

"I'm okay on the couch."

"It's just that I'm about to make some phone calls." Did that sound bossy or whiny? "Or I can work upstairs if you prefer."

He gave me a strange look, like "Who is this woman and what did you do with Kate Garrett?" I was wondering the same thing.

"I'll take you up on your offer. Thank you."

Getting along was exhausting.

"Shall I call you in a couple of hours?"

"Just in case I don't wake up?" He grinned. "Not bloody likely. In the army I learned how to sleep for exactly as long as I gave myself, and no longer."

I shrugged and turned back to my work, trying not to look at Carmedy's backside as he went up the stairs. Giving myself a mental shake, I told myself that looking was natural. By the time I allowed myself to appreciate the view, Carmedy was gone. Then I wondered, again, if I should offer the place to him. He might be able to live with the ghosts better than I could.

Speaking of ghosts, I had some reading to do. As soon as I got my calls out of the way, I curled up on the couch with a tablet.

12

Joe Garrett's Audio File Transcript

It's good to be working with Vince again. Marten had a family emergency and a homicide came up. Jewelry store heist gone wrong. There's something hinky about it. Just the kind of case I like to get my hands on.

Marten is smartening up. She's letting Women in Crisis do the social work and acting as backup in case things go south with the husband. I'm betting something happened at home that gave her a wakeup call. Maybe she realizes that other people depend on her to stay alive.

I've got Kate to remind me. She's already turning into a decent detective. I gave her a robbery scenario from my rookie detective days and she suspected fraud after the first read-through. Campbell and I pegged it for an inside job, but didn't see it was fraud until later.

I remembered that scenario. At the

time I felt like I was the smartest kid on the planet. Later I realized that my father had given me a clue that there was something unusual about the case. I just had to figure out what it was. He was better at faking me out by the time he told me about the jewellery heist.

In any case, I wasn't reading this to find out how proud my father was. I'd do that later. I skimmed down until I found a reference to Marten. It wasn't very long.

Damn! Why do they go back? I've got to touch base with Marten and makes sure she doesn't do anything stupid. Vince and I are preparing the jewelry store case for the arraignment. I can't hold her hand through this.

I assumed he was referring to Irene going back to her husband. Most people don't get why the abused went back to their abusers. They think in terms of verbal and physical assault. Assault can be traumatic, but it doesn't twist the victim inside, making them feel that they don't deserve anything better.

There were a few rants against rookie

detectives who get too emotionally involved interspersed throughout the murder case notes which was generously peppered with rants against people who felt they were entitled by status and education to ride roughshod over other people.

Coming from a long line of beat cops and factory workers, my father's metaphorical collar was as blue as they came.

I skimmed ahead.

"... Detective Marten and I are responding to an urgent personal plea from Mrs. Collins. She is trapped in the house. Evidently, she went back for her cat, not to stay, but her husband caught her. We're leaving Mohr outside as backup and tactical is on alert for the worst case."

"Do you always have a backup recorder running?"

"Not always. Forget about it. Keep your head in the game."

Bingo!

< *Noise* >

"Mrs. Collins? ... Irene?
< Noise >
"Irene? Are you in there?"
< 8 seconds >
< Noise >
< Noise >

Maybe a text transcript wasn't the best idea. Either that or I needed a more intuitive program. At least it timed the pauses but I wondered if there were clues to what was happening in the apparent silence.

< Bang >

It actually interpreted that.

< Noise >

But not that.

"We might as well go in now."

I'd bet lunch at Helios that was my father and he wasn't happy with Marten. Was she the one that shot? Or did she kick in the door after hearing a shot?

I continued reading.

< 6 seconds >

"Clear."

< 10 seconds >

< Bang >

"Step away from Irene, Mr. Collins. Now!"

"You have no right to enter my home without a warrant."

"Calm down, Mr. Collins. We came at your wife's invitation. We didn't enter until we heard the gun shot, which gave us reasonable cause. Now we find your wife on the floor with 2 big nails through her skirt."

"I was fixing a floor board. The stupid bitch got in my way."

"That's just…"

"Enough, Marten. Mr. Collins, please place the nail gun on the floor."

"Fuck off!"

"Now, Mr. Collins. While you are armed with a potentially deadly weapon, Marten might think you pose a danger. One wrong move–or something hinting of a wrong move– and she not only could shoot you, she'd be obligated to do so."

< 3 seconds >

"Seriously."

That's my dad. He always waited a three-count before adding "Seriously."

… Seriously.

< Noise >

< Noise >

"Stay down, Mr. Collins, on your knees, hands laced behind your head. Leave Mrs. Collins for now, Marten. Cuff Mr. Collins while I cover him."

< Noise >

"Mohr? We could use your help now. Marten, watch out! Collins, no!"

< Bang >

"Put the gun down. The next shot is going to go between your eyes."

"I'll kill her first. Put your gun down and I'll let go of your partner. I'll keep her gun until I'm safely away. You can even keep my bitch of a wife. Just lower your gun."

"Not going to happen."

< 3 seconds >

"Now, Mr. Collins."

< Noise >

"Ah, shit."

< Bang >

< Bang bang>

< Noise >

< Noise >

< Grunt >

"What the Sam hell! Joe?" That had to be Mohr.

< Jingle >

Jingle? What the hell was that?

"Get a compress on Joe's wound. Now Detective! Bloody rookies."

< Grunt >

"You can't leave me like this."

"Stay still. Your body weight is pushing that compress into your wound. Move and you'll bleed out."

< Grunt >

"Dispatch 10-52, officer down. Suspect wounded. 10-55 went south."

< Noise >

"Joe Garrett. GSW to hip."

< Noise >

"Yeah, Joe. Tell Thorsen."

< Noise >

"Two GSW just below the shoulder. Looks like Joe got him in the arm too."

< Noise >

"I'll check. I'll take over with Joe. You better put a dressing on Collins. Maybe you can get Mrs. Collins to stop keening too."

< Static >

"You awake Garrett? Don't go to sleep on the job."

"Hurts like hell."

"That'll teach you to only wing the guy."

"He was using Marten as a shield."

"What was that shit about putting the next one between his eyes?"

< Laugh >

< Cough >

"Fuck that hurts. Why the hell can't I pass out until the painkillers arrive?"

"Life sucks–"

< End session >

13

Hand shaking, I set aside the rest of the transcript.

I was at school when this happened. The Chief, though he wasn't chief at the time, called my mother and took her to the hospital. His wife, Aunt Maggie, came into my classroom. She taught–still teaches–at the high school I attended. Her face told me something was wrong and I expected the worst. As soon as I learned that my father was still alive and would probably remain so, I figured everything would be okay.

Of course, I was wrong.

Knowing something of what I might read next, I knew I couldn't handle it right now. Besides, I had more calls to make. Last thing I needed was Carmedy giving me a hard time about putting off my real work.

I had just finished building two cream

cheese and peach preserve sandwiches when Carmedy entered the office. He didn't look particularly rested, but I wasn't going to rock the boat by pointing this out.

"It's not as healthy as the meal you made me," I said, handing over the paper bag, "but they should help you get through the night. I've also made a thermos of cafe au lait and given you the last two energy drinks. I'll go shopping this evening."

"Don't get too much," he said. "Maggie and Igor will send us home with enough leftovers for a week and the office closes down in a couple of days."

"Speak for yourself, Carmedy. I'll be around to eat. Even if there's no work here, I have a ton of stuff to do upstairs."

Carmedy slung his pack on his shoulder, and patted his pockets for keys and wallet, then checked the heavy-duty flashlight on his belt. No gun.

No real need, but it didn't stop me from carrying my Sig Sauer and a Taser. Strict weapons controls only applied to law-abiding civilians and I was no civilian.

"I'm going home tonight if you want to use the apartment," I said.

He shook his head.

"I'm okay. I changed the sheets for you, by the way."

"Thanks. You didn't have to."

He shrugged and turned to go. Over his shoulder he said, "Yes, I did."

Too much information.

The plan was Carmedy would do a walk through the neighbourhood before it got dark, checking likely places for signs of a body dump or burial plot. Later he'd join the patrol and lend a fresh ear to the local gossip.

About the time he was patrolling, I'd start visiting suspects. That way, in the unlikely event there was trouble, he'd be in the neighbourhood to help out. Meanwhile, I had errands to run.

Although it was before six, I went upstairs to change out of day-wear. What with my closet purge, I now had as many usable clothes at the apartment as in my room at Magnus' place.

Before heading out, I ran through my checklist. Wallet, cuffs, Maglite and shopping bags were in my large shoulder bag. Keys, personal alarm and eCom went in my pockets. Taser and pistol had their respective holsters, out of sight thanks to my pea coat.

But it wouldn't be out of sight when I was visiting homes. Come to think of it, my father rarely went around armed as a private detective... unless you counted his walking stick, Maglite and utility knife.

I locked up my pistol and dropped my Taser into my purse.

A couple of hours later, with one bag full of wrapped presents and another with groceries, I hailed a taxi and headed home.

Magnus was still working nights. He left directions to a meatloaf and a container of marinated vegetables in the fridge and signed "Love M. PS: Fresh cookies in the tin."

I broke up a slice of the meatloaf over the vegetables and ate out of the container while I read police reports.

Blake Collins had three arrests for drunk and disorderly conduct and a sealed juvenile file. Police had been called out on noise complaints multiple times before the spousal abuse file was opened. Most of the time the violation was the result of partying too hard and too late with his cronies.

These parties were rowdy enough for the on-scene officer to scan IDs. Paulo Crabbe was one of the recurring names.

Another familiar name popped out: Koehne, Ishmael Micah. I knew two men by that name. Unsurprisingly, it was the younger Mr. Koehne who had been a troublemaker.

I loaded my map of the neighbourhood. The report put Crabbe on Orchard Road, same house he lived in now. Koehne junior resided on Side Road 6, which was now called Applegate Drive. I knew from the office leases, this was also the home address of Koehne senior. I added another "o" to my map.

Twenty minutes later, I asked the cabby to wait while I dropped off groceries at the office, bribing her with the promise of a peanut butter and peach jam sandwich.

Carmedy almost always made it in before I did and he'd want his energy drinks and fresh bagels waiting. On the way to East Hills, I called him.

14

"Hey, partner."

I smiled. He must be having a good evening if he was being so friendly.

"How's it going?" I asked.

"Nice night for a walk."

"I just wanted to give you a heads-up. I'm going to start interviewing the people on my list. I don't anticipate any trouble but…"

"Better safe than sorry, right?"

"That's what I always say," said Mrs. Parnell.

Carmedy must have put me on speaker.

"You never told me your partner was so good looking, Detective."

"I didn't want to make your husband jealous."

There was a deep chuckle I assumed was Carmedy.

"Ping my eCom with your location so I can find you if you shout," he said, then disconnected.

I uploaded the addresses I would be visiting and established a quick link to his eCom in case I needed to "shout" for help. Soon after, the taxi stopped. I filed the electronic receipt to recoverable expenses and wished the cabby a safe evening.

I planned to start with Mr. Crabbe. Since he wasn't home, my first interview was Irene Cole, formerly Collins.

No Christmas decorations adorned her property, but a tidy mulch covered path lined with solar lights led the way to the porch. Beside the door was a hand-painted sign advertising peach preserves for sale, by appointment only. The logo was very familiar.

I almost laughed when I connected the dots. Irene Koehne/Collins/Cole produced that delicious peach compote that Carmedy I had been enjoying for the last couple of days.

Here was a potential answer to Mr. Parnell's question of how Irene wound up with Blake Collins. He was a friend of her brother's.

I rang the bell.

No answer.

I rang again then knocked loudly on a panel of one-way glass set that decorated the heavy wood door.

"Who's there?" The voice came through the speaker by the door.

Knowing I was in full view of the unseen woman, I adopted an open stance and a friendly, but not too friendly, smile.

"I'm Kate Garrett, one of the detectives hired by your community to find the cat-killer."

"I don't belong to the neighbourhood watch."

"Understood, Ms. Collins, but you do like to walk at night. It is possible you've seen something without realizing it and I am sure you would want to help keep your neighbourhood safe. After all, people who hurt animals are just as likely to hurt humans."

There was a pause long enough to make me wonder if I should knock again.

"That doesn't follow," said Irene. "Being a butcher doesn't make you a suspect for cutting up human bodies. Exterminators don't become killers just because they destroy vermin."

Actually, a butcher might become a suspect if the cadaver was cut up like a side of beef and an exterminator would be questioned if their poisons matched the cause of death. I didn't argue the point.

"Your neighbours' pets are being targeted, not vermin or meat."

Another long pause.

"I never saw anything," she said finally. "Now please go."

I changed tack.

"You make that wonderful peach jam, don't you?"

"What does that have to do with cats?"

"Nothing, I just noticed your sign. Your brother rents an office suite from me. My partner and I bought some jars from him. It's delicious!"

"Are you going to evict my brother if I don't talk to you?"

"Uh, no," I said, momentarily derailed. "I would appreciate talking to you about your usual route when you walk, Ms. Collins. You might have noticed something without realizing it.

"While I'm here, I'd also like to pick up some of your peach chutney. However," now I laid on a tone of shocked affront, "I would never consider letting your lack of cooperation impact on a business relationship."

"You can't come in."

"I understand. We can talk like this."

She didn't say anything. I took her silence as consent.

"Graydon Parnell told me that your cat went missing a few years ago."

"Ten years ago. My husband killed her before he left." Her tone was flat, almost distant, as if she was speaking from far away and long ago.

"Was your husband often a violent man?"

"No," was her knee jerk reply. "Not physically," she said after a brief hesitation. "Not most of the time. He threatened violence to the things I loved, like Susie, my cat."

"Did he threaten your family?"

"My brother sometimes," she said and I could hear anger touch her carefully regulated tone.

"But your brother and he were friends."

"So? He said he loved me."

The anger was bubbling up. I waited, letting her fill the silence.

"He never threatened Mike when he was around. I don't know if he really would have hurt him, but he said he would if I didn't behave. I couldn't take the chance."

On top of physical and emotional abuse, Collins effectively held Irene's loved ones hostages. No wonder she resisted leaving him.

"Do you know where your husband went after he shot Detective Garrett?"

"Your name is Garrett," she said, sounding thoughtful. I hoped she wasn't thinking of telling me to go away.

"Joe Garrett was my father."

"He was very good to me. I felt safer when he was alive."

She gave a shaky sigh.

"To answer your question, I hope

Blake went to Hell and never comes back."

I gave her a moment before asking the next question.

"Do you think it's possible that he might have returned?"

This produced a pause so long, I wondered if she was still there. Then I heard her shaky sigh.

"I don't think my husband would return. I hope not. However, sometimes I fear he never left."

I turned the topic back to the present and what Irene's nightly routine was before I was hired. Twenty minutes later, I walked away with a little more information, four jars of chutney and a bottle of syrup.

The jars were delivered via a delivery door near the side entrance. It revealed a compartment with a closed door to the inside of the house. The jars were set out for me. She wouldn't take money for them–they were her gift for my father's sake–but I left my card with a note to call me if she thought of anything new.

Paulo Crabbe still wasn't home so I

went across the street to visit Theo Konstantin.

15

Mr. Konstantin must have been watching for me, because the lights went out when I reached his front walk. Knocking didn't work so I sat on his porch swing and waited. While I waited, I ran a police check.

It wasn't a deep search. It just looked for local interaction with City Police. Konstantin had never been arrested. He had no outstanding traffic or bylaw violations. What he did have was a three-page list of complaints against his neighbours.

The Johansson's were too noisy. The Georges let their dog run loose on his lawn. Mrs. Bailey, Mr. Bennett, Ms. McKenzie and Mrs. Gowda were all accused of verbal harassment.

The investigating constable noted on each report that harassment for Mr. Konstantin meant that someone stopped him on the street to talk.

The front door opened.

"If you don't leave, I'll call the police," said Konstantin, poking his head out.

"I am the police. I'm Detective Kate Garrett."

"Well in that case…"

Konstantin beckoned me into his living room and invited me to sit. I expected dark and dreary. Instead I found blinding white. Every paintable surface was white. The upholstery was white. My soft-soled shoes squeaked on white laminate floors.

"You keep a clean and bright house," I said.

"Easy to see when people break in."

"This happens often?"

Konstantin smirked.

"Not since I redecorated."

I took out my eCom to take notes and put Carmedy on standby. Mr. Konstantin was a loon.

"You're Joe Garrett's daughter."

I was only a little surprised. My father got around.

"How did you know my father?"

"I was his first client when he became

a private investigator. I hired him to look for my wife. The police said she deserted me. I was sure that she had run off with that Collins guy when he disappeared."

"Blake Collins?"

Konstantin made a face and spat on the floor. Then he carefully cleaned up after himself.

"That snake was always flirting with my wife... patting her on the back and letting his hand linger... telling me I should watch out if I wanted to keep her."

He started to spit again, paused and swallowed.

"What did my father find out?"

His righteous anger deflated. "He found her in Toronto, living with one of her college friends.

"She said she left me because I was paranoid. Then she said she would never have run off with Blake Collins. He was an evil man and she might have put up with my paranoia if I'd stopped him from harassing her." Then his anger erupted. "I ask you, is it paranoid when I'm right about people?"

By letting him catalogue all the people who he felt he was right about, I gave Konstantin a chance to calm down. There were a few I hadn't read about.

For instance, Paolo Crabbe was a walking odor violation besides being a noisy neighbour and inclined to walk the neighbourhood and pee on people's lawns. Almost all his neighbours poked their noses in where they didn't belong and someone was stealing his bandwidth.

As it turned out, Konstantin had been a frequent client of my Garrett Investigations and I soon identified him as the one my father called "Special K."

"Your father was the one who suggested the white décor as a deterrent."

Clever.

When Konstantin started winding down, I let him know I had other interviews to conduct.

On the porch, I messaged Carmedy, checked the power level on my Taser and the batteries in my Maglite. Mr. Konstantin watched me from the behind his transoms, giving me an approving nod every time I looked his way. When I looked back a last time, he added a salute.

I'd almost made it to Crabbe's door when Carmedy called.

"Leave your eCom open," he said.

"Why?"

"Mrs. Gowda is concerned for your safety."

Mrs. Gowda watched crime shows in her spare time. She especially liked *True Crime* and *Cop Shop*. This made her conversant with police technobabble and a bit of an armchair detective.

"She wanted to know if Mr. Crabbe was a suspect or a witness. I told her he was a person of interest."

"Let's hope he's a person of great interest," said Mr. Gowda over the speaker. "My Sandy is suffering extreme cabin fever, but I'm not letting him out at night until this case is solved."

"Sandy's your cat?" asked Carmedy

Mrs. Gowda and I replied in unison: "Husband."

"I'll leave the line open," I said. But I was going to mute the speaker. Otherwise I'd hear Mrs. Gowda's running commentary on the interview.

Crabbe answered the door in an orange kimono, worn open over pink satin boxers with a cherry-red lip-print design. Both looked like they might fall off his skeletally thin body.

I had a near overwhelming desire to tie his kimono shut with a granny knot.

"Good evening, Mr. Crabbe. I'm Detective Kate Garrett. I'm investigating the cat killing for the Neighbourhood Committee. Do you have time answer a few questions?"

He blinked at me a few times then snorted.

"You think I'm a suspect don't you?"

"Right now I'm just gathering information, sir."

"Come on in, honey. Meet my friends."

16

He ushered me through the vestibule, into his cluttered living room. I counted six cats. Three lounging on chairs, two stretched on under the glass-top coffee table, and a kitten peeking out of a toque on the floor.

"They're all rescues," he explained. "I'd have more but City Bylaw restricts me to six."

"You must love cats."

"Better than most people. For one thing, cats don't get bent out of shape when I make a joke. I'm betting you're here because I told Sandy Gowda that I was looking for a little pussy when he caught me on his property."

He pointed to the cat in the hat.

"That one got loose. There's always one in the bunch that wants to be an outdoor kitty, but I don't allow it."

He paused for effect.

"It's irresponsible."

He waved at the couch, which was the only cat-free seat in the room.

"Wanna beer? Something stronger?"

"Neither. Thank you."

"I'll get beer."

I removed my coat and draped it over the end of the couch and put my bag on the floor beside it. Crabbe returned, clutching two bottles. I shook my head at his renewed offer and sat at the edge of the couch, within easy reach of my things.

Crabbe lounged sideways, one leg on the floor, the other crooked and leaning against the back. If I cared to, I could look up his shorts in this position.

Only years of training stopped me from shuddering. Instead I asked about his cats.

"Are they all tagged and chipped?"

"They don't have to be. They're indoor animals. Cats would be a lot better off if the law had made letting your pets loose illegal instead of going the electronic chip route."

I felt a soapbox rant coming on.

"A chip isn't going to stop your cat getting or spreading rabies or feline distemper or heart worm. It won't stop your cat from getting run over or poisoned either."

He shook his head. "But I might have to tag junior. She's a tricky kitty."

I asked him whether he had seen anyone or anything suspicious on his evening walks.

He went into exhaustive detail that amounted to him seeing nothing useful. When I asked him about strays in the neighbourhood, he was more helpful.

"I pick 'em up when I can. If I can't keep 'em or find 'em a home there are always farmers looking for more vermin hunters. Better that than waiting for execution in a small cage."

I took issue with his portrayal of Animal Control's operation. They worked with the Humane Society to return or place domestic animals as much as possible.

I kept my thoughts to myself and let him vent until he reached for the second beer. Then I turned the conversation.

"I understand you knew Blake Collins."

He paused, bottle tilted.

"We hung around together when we were younger. Why?"

"It's been suggested that he wasn't fond of cats and might have abused his wife's cat. It's not a strong lead, but if he came back…"

Crabbe gave a snort of laughter.

"He got along fine with my cats. He was just yanking her chain."

He leaned back and gulped down almost half the bottle as if to make up for the brief pause in his drinking.

"Blake was a man's man. He was hetro when it came to sex, but he preferred the company of his buddies. Back then I was one of them. Never could understand why he married. Now me, I like to stay available."

Crabbe started to spread his legs so his boxers would gap more. I countered with another question.

"What about Koehne?"

"Mike "call me Ishmael" Koehne? Bit of a loser, but Blake let him hang out with us. We stay in touch, go out for a beer or six. You don't think he could be an animal killer, do you? He's so squeamish he faints at the sight of blood. Blake showed me a couple of times."

He cupped his crotch. "I could make you faint."

The man was an idiot.

"I should go, Mr. Crabbe."

I handed him my business card before standing and putting on my coat.

"If you think of anything else…"

He squinted at the card then turned it over and over.

"Garrett. Any relation to Joe Garrett?"

Since I was a kid, I had taken it on faith that everyone in the City knew my father. Today was proving I was right.

"He's my father. How did you know him, Mr. Crabbe?"

"Call me Paulo."

He levered himself off the couch.

"You got to stay for a drink now. I was outta town when he died. Would have been at the service if I'd been around."

Crabbe weaved out of the room, avoiding cats, cat toys and other things that landed on the floor and stayed there.

He returned through the obstacle course with two very full shot glasses. Miraculously, very little of the amber liquid left the glasses. He passed me the fullest one.

"We'll toast you father."

I could almost feel my father rolling over in his grave. "Never accept a drink that's already been poured." He'd drilled that into me since I was ten. Of course, he meant any drink, not just alcoholic. Even so, I took the proffered glass and raised it for a toast.

"Here's to Joe Garrett," said Crabbe. He tossed down his shot. "May he rot in hell for his sins."

The glass was at my lips, which was as far I intended it to go. With snake-like speed, Crabbe leaned in and tipped the contents into my mouth. I tried to spit, but he covered my mouth and soon I could feel the telltale burn at the back of my throat. Then he pushed me onto the couch, landing on top of me. Air whooshed out of me, spraying the liquor I managed not to swallow in Crabbe's face.

As soon as I got my breath back, I pushed him off of me, onto the floor.

"Crap! What the fuck was that about?"

He just laughed and pushed himself up to sit on the floor between the couch and the coffee table. A black and white cat came out from under the table to check on him. Laughter morphed to cooing noises as he fussed over the animal.

Whatever he'd spiked my drink with was going to work fast. I could feel the lethargy spreading. Soon I was going to either fall forward on to the floor or back into the deep cushions of the couch.

"That's right. Go to sleep Garrett Junior. I couldn't touch Garrett Senior for what he did to Blake, but I sure can touch you."

"What is your problem? Collins shot my father. My father winged him, but he was well enough to bolt."

"So his whore partner hunted him down. Garrett either sent her or covered up for her. Then he retired with a full pension and honours heaped on him."

He put the cat down and started to get up. I smashed the heel of my fist into the top of the coffee table. Both of us were surprised when the glass shattered, but not as much as the cats that went from zero to speed blur before the first shard hit the floor.

"Sit! Stay!"

I was always better with dogs than cats.

"Bitch!"

I grabbed my bag and stood, only a little wobbly. He didn't move until I started backing towards the door. Then he was up– and his boxers were down. He stumbled. I reached into my bag and grabbed what I thought was my Maglite. When righted his self, I slammed the peach syrup into his face.

That's when the door burst open.

17

"Kate!"

Through the open door, lights were flashing. They made my head spin. The effects of pain and adrenaline were subsiding and the drug was taking hold of me again.

Carmedy caught me before I fell. My last thought before passing out was if he insisted on calling me Kate, I'd have to start calling him Jake.

I woke up in the ER with Mohr staring down at me.

"About time, Garrett. The shot they gave you was supposed to wake you up five minutes ago."

"I guess I needed the rest."

My head was clearer. I hurt all over. I was hooked up for plasma, oxygen and who knows what drugs, and my hand was enveloped in what looked like a Mylar balloon.

No surprise there. This was a

standard field dressing that combined compression and cushioning when a wound had foreign objects in it. It kept everything clean and secure until the patient could be treated.

I waved my balloon.

"This doesn't hurt as much as I think it should."

"Topical analgesic," said Mohr. "It'll hurt like a bitch later."

"How's Crabbe?"

"Broken nose."

"No cuts?"

"Nothing serious. But then he didn't put his fist through glass."

"Worked though," said Carmedy–that is–Jake, giving my shoulder a pat. I hadn't seen him there on the other side of the bed. "Did Joe tell you about using pain to counteract a tranquilizer?"

"Not exactly." They were going to laugh at me. "I saw it in on the Avengers–the British spy series not the American superhero franchise."

"Haven't seen that," said my partner. "I guess Joe hadn't got around to introducing me to that show."

"It's a good one," said Mohr. "I think I remember the episode."

I should have known. Some people bonded over sports. Dad hosted vidnights of old crime shows served with appropriate food and drinks.

Since I was pretty young when we did the Avenger's marathon, Dad made a champagne glass fountain with sparkling grape juice. We fenced with umbrellas and I learned how to throw a hat like a Frisbee. Good times.

Mohr pinched my arm.

"Don't fall asleep, Garrett. I need to take your statement."

I nodded and looked over at my partner. "Can you go check on Crabbe?"

"I was going to stick around so you wouldn't have to do this twice."

"I'd really appreciate it Jake."

He looked stunned. It was as if I'd never used his first name before. I'm pretty sure I used it once–maybe twice.

He gave my shoulder another squeeze and left the cubicle.

Mohr pulled up a stool and sat down. "What?"

"I need to ask you something personal before I give my statement."

Mohr turned his eCom towards me. Then he held it closer when it was obvious I was having trouble focussing.

"Recording is on standby. I guessed there was something when you dismissed the soldier."

He leaned in to whisper. "Is he getting in your face too much?"

"Huh? No."

"He's got awfully protective of you."

"He probably thinks my father expects it of him."

Mohr shook his head and I was curious about what he thought, but I also knew I might not have much time before we were interrupted.

"You remember when my father was shot in the hip?"

"I won't forget that day. I should have gone in earlier."

"You didn't know." My response was automatic. The fact is, I don't know if he should have anticipated events or not. I'm not sure I would have in his place. "It doesn't matter now."

Mohr nodded.

"Joe always said you can't change the past. You can only learn from it."

"The past has just bitten me in the ass. Crabbe thinks Blake Collins is dead, that Dad's partner Marten killed him, and Dad covered it up."

Mohr gave a snort of disgust. "Crabbe's an idiot."

"He was so convinced, he assaulted me for revenge."

He rolled his eyes. "It doesn't make it so. Anyway, Carmedy knows all this. He recorded it."

"Yes, but. . ." How could I explain this? "I knew my father back then. Carmedy didn't. I know what the injury did to him and how angry he was."

"I knew him too."

"That's why I'm asking for your help, Mohr, not Carmedy's. Two people disappeared after the shooting."

"Marten resigned. With good reason."

I gave him the long stare. It was actually kind of fun putting him at the receiving end of it.

"No, I didn't see her after she handed

in her resignation."

I waited.

"Okay, Garrett, I'll see what I can find that you can't on your own." He switched on his recorder. "Now, in your own words, what happened when you visited Mr. Crabbe."

Jake returned while I was describing how things went south after I gave Crabbe my card. I did my best to ignore him and how he might feel about the lash out against my father. I had to focus on presenting the facts, clearly and succinctly.

When I was done, Mohr asked, "Where was your service pistol?"

"Locked up at home." I flushed with embarrassment as Mohr played the staring game with me. "I'm on leave. I'm not required to carry. And I thought it would be better if I didn't push the fact I'm a cop when I'm working as a PI."

He frowned.

"Ca-Jake doesn't carry a gun." Okay. That sounded a bit whiny.

"Ca-Jake isn't a cop. He's a combat

veteran who could probably kill that wiry perve with his bare hands."

Mohr took a deep breath. He reached for his eCom, possibly thinking he should record over this altercation, but pulled his hand back. "No offense, Carmedy."

"None taken. You are correct. I could have killed that parasite with my bare hands and was even tempted to do so."

He was in "soldier reporting" mode. I'd seen it before. Not only did he stand at attention, he seemed to lose the ability to use contractions.

"Point of information, a gun is an artillery piece. I do carry a sidearm when the situation warrants it. I prefer an assault rifle, however."

"You see?" said Mohr. "He's a PI, but he'll always be a soldier. And you, Garrett, will always be a cop. So act like one."

"Sorry," I said. And I was. I could tell that I had worried both of them and really, I should have been able to handle Crabbe better.

Mohr nodded and turned off the recorder. "Joe always said: "Don't be sorry, just don't do it again."″

If I had a fiver for every time someone started a sentence with "Joe always said," I'd be a thousand dollars richer by now.

"Are you really going to include that in your report?" I asked, nodding towards Mohr's eCom.

"Nah. I just kept it going so I could play it for the Chief. If he knows I chewed you out, he won't feel the need.

"I'm going to go print up your statement. Don't leave the hospital before I get you to sign off on it."

As soon as he was gone, Jake nabbed the stool and sat.

"Crabbe is okay. They're keeping him overnight. The assault has been recorded on two devices…"

"Three. Maybe four." I counted off on my good hand. "My eCom, your eCom and then, from the moment I said "crap" Emergency Response Coordination was uploading my recording and linked to my eCom."

"And four?"

"I have a feeling Mohr has a flag on me. I wouldn't put it past him to acquire a copy of the ERC recording as they received it."

"That's legal?"

I shrugged.

"I'm not a private citizen, so yes. It's not exactly kosher and both the Chief and Staff Sergeant in charge would raise hell if it went beyond him, but Mohr was my mentor. He's expected to look out for me."

"And I thought platoons were close knit." Jake shook his head like he was trying to knock his thoughts back into place. "Oh, and if he starts calling me Ca-Jake on a regular basis, I will take it out on you."

I started to protest but caught on he was joking. Maybe I was getting better at reading him. Or maybe it was hard to believe he was angry when he was holding my good hand. I really did worry him. Thank heavens he kept voice business-like.

"So, do you still think Crabbe could be the cat-killer?"

I shook my head.

"Not impossible, but not likely either.

I'm not even sure I'd characterize him as a Peeping Tom anymore."

"You didn't buy his searching for his pussy cat line did you?"

"No. I just think he's more of an exhibitionist. He wants to be seen." I shuddered. "I wish I could take back what I saw of him."

Jake said nothing but I could hear his teeth grind. I changed the topic.

"It's hard to pin down who is killing the cats when we don't know why they're doing it. Mr. Konstantin might think the cats are out to get him. Crabbe might be punishing the cat owners for letting their cats out."

"Graydon Parnell might be killing cats because he can't kill his wife," said Carmedy.

I grinned and shook my head.

"He really loves his wife. Just don't tell him I shared that with you."

"Someone might just be doing it because they can."

Again, I shook my head, more gently this time because it was starting to hurt.

"There has to be a reason. We just

have to find it."

"Crazy doesn't need a reason," said Jake, poking my balloon hand.

"Crazy always has a reason. It just doesn't have to make sense."

18

December 21

I woke up when the painkillers wore off. I was in my father's bed. My pills and a bottle of water were on the bedside table. I still had my underpants on and Jake's shirt. He gave me the shirt off his back because they had to cut mine off. Everything else I had been wearing, including my bra, was in the laundry hamper.

Interesting, since I didn't remember getting out of the car.

I was dead tired when they released me from the ER. Even with the whole blood they gave me after removing the glass and sticking me back together, I felt like I was down a litre.

As soon they finished pumping blood and antibiotics into me, I was released into Jake's care. Once we decided he should take me to Dad's apartment, I must have dozed off. That's the last thing

I remember from that very long night.

When I got around to going downstairs, it was mid-afternoon. I found Jake on the office couch reading. I poured some juice and opened up my mail.

"Check it later," he said, coming up behind me. "Tell me about the Collins case–while you make coffee, of course."

This was easier said than done with one good hand. I directed Jake to rinse and fill the reservoir and to warm the carafe. I muddled through the bean related tasks on my own.

"Irene Collins is the peach jam lady," I said, once I'd counted the scoops for the grinder.

"No way."

"Way."

I picked up a half-empty jar and showed him Irene Cole's name in the fine print.

"Irene Cole, nee Irene Koehne, was married to Blake Collins. She changed her name to Cole, probably to distance herself from what happened."

"Does that mean you've dismissed her

as a suspect? After all, we don't want to stop our supply of preserves."

He was joking, but I was serious when I shook my head.

"Collins persecuted his wife. One of the ways he used was threatening her cat. Maybe he's come back. Ms. Collins says she's in terror of him returning and I believe her."

"What if Crabbe is right and he's dead?"

"That wouldn't matter if she didn't know or didn't believe it to be true."

I poured my black coffee and heated milk for Jake's latte. Pouring the two together into his mug was beyond my current capabilities, so I instructed him how to do it.

"Go slowly and pour each liquid at the same rate."

When that task was completed, I headed for the couch. I curled up at one end while Jake sat on the other. For a minute or two we savoured our drinks. Then Jake got back to business.

"What I meant was if Collins is dead, he can't be the cat killer. If he's alive, there's no reason for him to come back when he faces prosecution."

"Does he? My father, the man he shot, is dead. He might think he can come back now. According my father's files, he wasn't too bright."

Jake nodded, giving away that he'd been reading the transcripts I made. For a moment I was pissed off, but the drugs in my system slowed down my knee jerk reaction, giving me time to think.

My father was his partner. He had as much right as I did to read those files.

"There's another possibility," I said. "The fear he might come back may have triggered a psychotic break. Irene might have become her own tormentor."

"Even if she has, that doesn't mean she's going out at night killing cats."

"I'm just raising possibilities."

Jake blew out a sigh, or perhaps he was cooling his latte.

"We're back to where we were last night. Too many theories, not enough answers."

He had a point, but I had a gut feeling that Irene and her sociopathic husband were connected to the cat killings. Even if they weren't, there was a mystery there that needed to be solved.

"You've got a point," I said, getting up. "We're just going to keep going around in circles until we have another piece of the puzzle. I'm going to finish formatting the last section report. That sucker is going out before I leave the office."

"Can you handle that on pain meds and using only one hand?"

"One hand, a thumb and a finger."

He gave me the long stare. Honestly, I wished my father hadn't taught that trick to all his protégés. Fortunately, my mother taught me a counter attack. Roll your eyes heavenward, sigh and wait. Jake gave in first.

"Okay. I'm going home for a shower and clothes for tonight. Do you need me to pick up anything for you?"

I shook my head.

"Then I'll be back in time to sign off on the report before we go to the Thorsens."

I gave him a thumbs-up with my

bandaged hand.

Damn! I'd forgotten it was Yuletide.

As soon as Jake was gone I called Magnus. I needed the presents I'd left at his place and something festive from my closet.

"I can put it together, sweetie, but can I send it over in a taxi? I just got in and I'm toast."

"No problem."

Twenty minutes later there was someone at the door. I assumed it was the taxi driver but checked just in case. It was Mr. Koehne. Tempted as I was to ignore him, I was his landlord.

I opened the door halfway. I wasn't going to invite him in if I could avoid it.

"How can I help you, Mr. Koehne?"

His face was flushed and his fists were clenched at his sides.

"Is there something wrong?" I prompted.

"Stay away from my sister. She isn't well. She can't handle visitors."

"I was warned that she has issues dealing with people face to face. That's why we talked through her intercom."

Koehne's clenched fists came up in a defensive posture.

"I don't want you talking to her at all."

I took a half step back, not because he scared me but so I could slam the door in his face if he got any more belligerent.

"Mr. Koehne, I am conducting an investigation on behalf of the City Police and the East Hills Neighbourhood. I will talk to whoever I need to. Your sister didn't have an issue with this."

"You don't know what my sister has issues with." He dropped his fists and tried a different approach. "If you have any questions, please bring them to me. My sister isn't well. She's phobic."

That was a familiar line.

"What is she afraid of?"

I was damned sure if the answer didn't include her brother, he wanted it too.

"I don't know. Everything."

"What are you afraid of?"

Koehne tried to shove the door open. Big mistake. When I opened it halfway, I engaged the security lock that would keep it no more than halfway open. When he tried to push past me, I closed the door, trapping him between the jam and the edge.

Now the door wouldn't open further without me disengaging the lock. But it could close.

"Mr. Koehne, forceful entry unless you have due cause, is against the law. Now, I will excuse your transgression on the basis of brotherly concern, but only if you cooperate with my investigation."

He tried to wiggle free. I pushed the door, closing it a little bit more.

"Fine," he wheezed. "Just let me loose."

"No problem. Just back into the lobby and take a seat."

I released the door. At that moment the elevator door opened. It was Magnus.

Koehne looked like he wanted to make a run for it.

"Lim, help Mr. Koehne to a seat. Maybe he'll cooperate with an active duty police detective."

Magnus shot me a wide-eyed look,

but fell into the character of his twin brother easily.

"Do what Garrett tells you and don't make me take a professional interest in this."

He then stood by and looked grim. I just hoped that Koehne thought the large rolling suitcase he was pulling was filled with ordinance instead of wardrobe choices and Yuletide presents.

19

"I was asking your sister about her ex-husband. Do you know where Blake Collins is?

"No."

"Do you know what happened to him?"

He hesitated for a moment. "No. I haven't seen him since the day he made bail. My father was pissed that I helped him find a bonds broker but he was my friend. I didn't know then what he had been doing to my sister."

That was hard to believe. "You had no idea he was an abusive spouse?"

"Irene was really sensitive. I figured it was her imagination. It wasn't like she had bruises or anything. She used to think Blake would hurt me and that was just stupid."

I leaned against the door jam. This was a stupid time and place to interrogate him. I was too tired to follow through.

"Is Blake Collins the cat-killer?"

"No." Emphatic, quick and to the point, that was no lie.

"Do you know who is?"

"Why ask me? This is harassment."

"No," said Magnus, sounding like he was ready to spit gravel. "But I think Mr. Koehne has answered enough questions for tonight, Garrett."

Koehne was smart and made a hasty exit. As soon as he was gone I sank into one of the foyer chairs.

"I thought you were going to send the stuff by taxi?"

"I got a message from a friend in ER. I thought I better check up on you. Good job too."

"You were great. Thanks."

He shook his head. "That's not what I mean."

I looked down at my hand. Blood had soaked through the bandages. It was time for Magnus to take a professional interest in me.

A couple of hours later, clean, dressed in holiday casual wear and terrified, I stood in front of the Thorsens' house.

Think of it as a business function, I told myself. My business partner and I were meeting a client and his family for dinner. No reason to be stressed.

Right, except that the Thorsens were my family. I babysat the Thorsen kids. I was with Aunt Maggie when Erica, their youngest, was born. Up until Jake Carmedy came along, Dad and I spent every Yule at the Thorsen home. Then my father practically adopted Carmedy. After one very tense Yule dinner, I made a point of making the holiday visit with my mother and David for a couple of years and any time I might run into Jake. It was like I lost the Thorsens in a divorce.

The heavy hand of Jake landed on my shoulder. He had been parking the car.

"You okay?" he asked.

"Sure. I was just waiting for you."

"Liar."

The front door opened and the youngest Thorsen ran out and flung herself at me.

"Katie!"

The girl was no featherweight. She

almost knocked me off me feet. That would have been embarrassing: detective bowled over by ten-year-old.

"Erica! Settle down," the Chief shouted from the entry.

"It's okay. I don't mind."

I flipped the girl over. Erica giggled so hard she started to hiccup. I put her down and handed her two of the three bags I brought.

"Here monster-girl, these are to go under the tree."

Once Erica was out of sight, I hugged my bad hand to my chest. I was going to need more painkillers.

The Chief greeted me with a scowl.

"Mohr tell you about last night?"

"Only after I grilled him."

"Mohr didn't call you?"

"No. I called Mohr when my daily reports flagged your name. Why didn't you call me, Kathleen?"

"She was asleep," said Jake. "I should have called you, but it was a long night. Sorry about that Chief"

The Chief dropped an arm around my shoulder and guided me into the kitchen.

"We'll talk about it later. Tonight is Yuletide and work gets left at the door."

20

Aunt Maggie greeted me with the cook's hug. Her arms held me tight while she did her best to keep her hands off me. Andrea, the eldest, was scooping the dressing out of the turkey. She smiled and waved at us. Sonia had the job of stirring the gravy, so we exchanged a one-armed hug.

I brought premium coffee beans, Bailey's and peach chutney. Jake brought warm from the oven rolls, a pot of fresh churned butter and a jar of peach jam.

As soon as these contributions were presented, Maggie put us to work. "Igor is preparing to carve. Kate, can you set out the condiments and relishes? Or will the jars be a problem?"

I waved my good hand.

"I'm good."

"Jake, you know where to find the bread basket. What kind of rolls did you make us this year?"

"Multigrain harvest rolls and sour dough twists."

Jake baked bread? If it was good, I might cheat on my favourite bakery.

"Did you churn the butter?" I asked, setting out bowls for the pickles.

"I got it from a Mennonite farmer at the market."

"But you found time to bake bread between leaving the office and when you picked me up."

"From dough I prepped earlier and froze." He handed the bread basket to Erica to put on the table and helped me with the jar lids which, quite frankly, I didn't have a hope of wrestling open. "But that's why I was a bit late. Good job Lim was there to help out."

Magnus had cleaned and redressed my wound and was helping me wash and change when Jake arrived.

Since I didn't have enough energy to go upstairs, this was being done in the office washroom with the door open.

I reintroduced the two men who had met briefly at my father's memorial. They acted cool, but I got the impression they were measuring each other up.

Magnus had height.

Jake had depth.

I called it a tie but kept my mouth shut.

"He's a nurse," I reminded Jake.

"Are you two talking shop?" Igor growled, waving the carving knife at us.

"No!" we said together, making the kids laugh.

Once the pickles were out, I ferried the dishes to the table while Jake cleaned up.

There were two varieties of pickled onion, three varieties of pickled herring, gherkins, bread and butter pickles, sliced dill pickles, tamarind sauce, fig sauce and peach chutney.

I tested the chutney before bringing a couple of jars. It wasn't as good as the jam, but it was pretty damned good. Good enough to steal another taste.

"You like it?" Jake asked, catching me in the act. "Mrs. Cole must go through bushels of peaches. You have to wonder what she does with all the pits. Compost or recycling?"

"Mulch. But that's just the shells." Then I had an idea. "I need to check something."

"Not work," Jake warned, keeping his voice down. "Not here."

He followed me back to the kitchen, where I grabbed my bag and helped myself to a glass of water.

"Be right back, Aunt Maggie."

I headed for the powder room. I had one more task to heap upon Mohr, which, if it got back to the Chief would get me in more trouble than doing a little work at a family dinner. Besides, I also needed to take painkillers and it was always a good idea to pee before dinner.

The Thorsens knew how to host a dinner. They had a buffet with a warming tray set up with a plate of dark meat, a plate of white meat, two types of potatoes, three hot vegetables, gravy and stuffing. Then there was an ice tray with a mixed green salad, the assortment of pickles and herring. I knew what was coming and had worn harem pants with a drawstring waist.

"Red or white?" the Chief asked, as I loaded up my plate.

"Neither," said Jake. "She's on prescription pain meds for a couple of days."

"Traitor."

"Good call," said Maggie. "If you don't have wine, you should okay for a little something later."

After the main course, I made Irish Coffees and we settled in the living room. There was an open spot on the couch next to Jake and I was tempted to take it. Then Erica pulled me down onto the floor next to her.

A moment later, excited little girl bounced up again, like she was made of rubber—a trait she'd had since she was a toddler.

"Presents!" she cried. "I want to give Kate my present first."

No one objected, so Erica dug through the parcels until she found what she was looking for. Finally, she handed over a homemade box with a recycled bow on top. I opened the box, removed the tissue and pulled out a coffee mug. It was a bit lumpy and included a perfect thumb impression where the handle was joined to the cup.

"I made it myself," Erica said. "I painted this side."

She pointed to the side nearest me. It was decorated with holly and mistletoe.

"But on this side," she turned the mug in my hands, "I had them put a photo. See there's me."

It was a family photo from Erica's first year. She was more interested in trying to get into Mama's blouse than posing for the camera. The Chief had Sonia on his lap. Beside him was Dad with Andrea perched on a knee.

On the other side of Maggie, I was trying to get baby Erica's attention. Beside me, sitting on the arm of the couch was Jake.

Our first and last Yule together, captured on a mug.

I felt a lump rise up in my throat. Behind me, I felt a knee press against my back, offering support. I knew it was

Jake's and leaned into it.

"You okay, Katie?" Erica asked, her voice trembling. "Don't you like it?"

I pulled the girl into a tight hug.

"I love it, honey. It's the best gift ever."

Erica returned the hug then went back to delivering presents, taking time out only when she found a present for herself.

I kept leaning against Jake's leg. When the kids went to play with their presents, I scooted back so my back was supported by the couch. Jake's knees kept me from tipping over. I was at that stage of drowsiness when I could hear conversations but didn't have the energy to respond or even to keep my eyes open.

"Big change from last time you two were in this house," said the Chief. "I take it you're getting along now."

"Except when we aren't," said Jake.

"I'm going to want her back, you know. I let her have the time off because she would have quit on me if I didn't, but she has the makings of a fine homicide detective. She won't get that opportunity in private investigation."

"Joe did."

"Joe was Joe. There's still a lot of resentment towards private contractors. You don't see it because Joe was practically legendary.

"In other cities there's been trouble. Toronto's given up the practice completely. They'll refer qualified private investigators, but they won't hire consulting detectives."

"Are you telling me that Carmedy and Garrett Investigations can't expect much work from you?" Jake asked. "Or will you still send us the pet crimes?"

Yay Jake, I thought.

"No business tonight," said Maggie, sounding as sleepy as I felt. "Jake, Andrea made up the couch in the basement. I was thinking Kate could sleep with the girls."

"I can sleep on the couch too," I said, without lifting my head. "It's big enough. Then Sonia won't have to share with Erica."

I opened my eyes and had the satisfaction of seeing my godfather blush. My guess was that it had more to do with being overheard than my provocative offer.

With a grunt of effort, I stood, using Jake's knee for leverage. Once I was up, I grabbed Jake's wrist and pulled him to his feet.

"Come on, partner. Good night all."

As promised, the couch was made up into a queen-sized bed. There was also a full bath. I called dibs on the basis that I couldn't keep standing much longer. One of my gifts had been a snowman nightshirt which I changed into after a quick wash up. When I came out, Jake had stripped down to t-shirt and boxers.

"Is sleeping with me a form of rebellion?"

I grinned.

"Partly."

"Hold that thought. I've had to pee for half an hour but I didn't want to disturb you."

While he was gone, I slipped between the covers, staying to the edge, leaving him most of the mattress. If we kept to the edges, we'd have a decent buffer zone. That would work.

I checked my eCom. I wasn't expecting anything from the lab this soon, I was happy to see a message from Mohr. I was going to owe him bigtime for this.

Jake emerged from the bathroom.

"You were saying."

"The Chief's right. We can't count on getting high profile cases. We may get called in for support, but we won't get the kind of cases my father got–not at first. The thing is, the first thing my father taught me was that the most important thing about solving a case was solving it. If you can take the stand in court and present the facts clearly, so that no one can shake your testimony, then you've done your job–whether it's a high-profile homicide or a traffic accident."

Jake looked sceptical, but I knew my father had said something similar to him.

"Okay," was all he said before turning off the light and taking the opposite edge of the bed.

Then he turned toward me, propping himself up on his elbow. "You've solved the case."

"No, not that," I said grinning up at

him in the dark. "But I now know where the bodies are buried."

21

December 22

"Kathleen Margaret Garrett!"

"We better get up," said Jake. "The Chief sounds like an angry thunder god."

We were back-to-back in bed. I was warm and comfortable and really wanted five more minutes like this. Maybe ten if my bladder held out.

"Do you want to the bathroom first?"

What a gentleman.

"Go ahead. I can wait. Besides, I think the Chief wants to yell at me right now."

I was pretty sure the only reason my godfather hadn't come downstairs to shout at me was because he was afraid that Jake and I would be doing something he didn't want to see.

Our night had been completely platonic. He didn't need to know that, which was one of the reasons I didn't bother getting dressed. I decided to face the music with bed head and jolly snowmen.

Naturally that meant the Chief had company.

"Good look for you, Garrett."

"Good morning to you too, Mohr."

"Sit! You too, Constable."

We sat at the kitchen table as ordered. It was round but the Chief managed to look as if he were at the head of it anyway.

"I understand that Mohr has been helping you with your investigations. I wasn't aware he had been seconded to Carmedy and Garrett Investigations."

"You did say I could have some police support."

The Chief growled but Mohr interrupted.

"Your understanding is incorrect, sir. I was following up on my own case that overlaps Garrett's."

"Are you turning lawyer on me, Constable?"

Mohr gave the Chief the stare. Few officers would be so brave.

"Chief, you are my superior in rank, but I'm not one of your detectives. I'm a community cop. One of my jobs is to prevent crime, or at least prevent it from escalating. So, when Mr. Crabbe sexually harassed and physically assaulted Garrett, it was my job to follow up.

"Garrett did ask me to keep one aspect of the situation confidential as long as possible. I think you'd agree we don't want one of our own being slandered. Joe was one of our own at the time of the crime he was being accused of."

Jake walked in at this point. The Chief waved in the direction of the coffee carafe. First, Jake put a hooded jacket over my shoulders. It was one of his, so I was able to put my bandaged hand through the sleeve without discomfort.

"Do you know about this, Jacob?"

Jake brought the carafe and four mugs to the table.

"I know about the accusation. Cream anyone?"

"I don't take cream," said Mohr.

"We don't have cream," said the Chief. "Only milk."

"Then I won't take milk." He pulled a black coffee towards him and pushed one to me. "Can I continue Chief?"

"Go ahead."

"Crabbe is convinced that Joe was complicit in the murder of his friend, Blake Collins–the guy that shot Joe, in case you forgot."

The Chief growled. "I wouldn't forget."

"His evidence is mostly circumstantial, with a side order of hearsay. The one thing he witnessed was Detective Marten leaving with Collins and his wife in the car witnesses saw Collins pack earlier. Since he was so sure Marten was in control, he didn't think it worthwhile to figure out where they went."

Mohr smirked. "Last night I asked Crabbe if he knew where Collins would go, if he was the one in control."

That's what I messaged Mohr about last night. His reply was: "DTYGTSE." Don't Teach Your Grandmother To Suck Eggs. I had no idea how old Mohr was, but he had the soul of a man two generations older.

"As soon as I left Crabbe, I called

Ziggy."

"So he could call in Nelly," said the Chief, only his usual gruff now.

Jake nudged me.

"Ziggy is a field geek," I explained. "His Uncle Mort is a dog trainer and handler. Nelly is his cadaver dog."

"A Human Remains Detection dog," said Jake. "I've worked with them in the past."

I shook my head. "Mort is old school and calls a cadaver a cadaver."

"Mort and Nelly will be arriving here…" Mohr checked his watch. "Any time now."

I looked at the Chief. He nodded and I rushed downstairs to dress. Since rushing is relative when you're a bit dopy from painkillers, I wasn't out of earshot when Mohr announce to my godfather and partner: "She still looks cute first thing in the morning."

22

Jake brought my coffee downstairs and found me struggling with my bra.

I had been prepared enough to bring some day clothes with me in case I stayed over. The denim joggers were a bit casual for day wear, but I just had to pull them on. The tunic was loose and flowing and dressed the outfit up a bit, but I couldn't put it on until I untangled my bra.

"Can you help me out?"

This was a two handed-operation and I was down a hand.

He sighed and set down the coffee. I almost told him that he didn't have to if I was too much trouble. Once again, the pain meds kept me from jumping to the wrong conclusion.

"I'm just one of the guys to you, aren't I?"

"Huh?"

He turned me so he could get at the back of my bra where it had rolled up into an uncomfortable twist. He undid the back, smoothed out the stretch fabric and hooked me up again. A hundred years of progress and bras still did up with a hook and eye fasteners.

"What do you mean, "One of the guys."?" I asked.

He eased the sleeve of my tunic over my bandaged hand. Then I pushed my other arm through before Jake pulled the garment over my head.

"I mean, you don't see me as a man."

"Actually, sometimes you remind me of my mother."

With something between a laugh and huff, he sat heavily on the bed. I sat down beside him.

"I'm trying to treat you like my partner, like I treat Valerio and Mohr–who only saw me first thing in the morning because I fell asleep on the locker room couch. How would you like me to treat you?"

"Like that but…"

I didn't find out what the "but" was. The Chief bellowed down the stairs that Mort and Nelly had arrived.

I called dibs on the Mort-mobile. Mort could only take one non-canine passenger in his customized HUV. That meant I could avoid lectures or questions for ten minutes. That was all the time it took reach the area where Stinktown bordered on the corridor of naturalized greenspace that divided it from one of the University's fields. By any other name, it was a hedgerow. Industrial farming had eliminated most of them. Eco-farming brought them back.

Stinktown was one of the sanctioned shanty towns that ringed the city. Its name came from the odor emitted by the City's Recycling Centre's methane plant. No one wanted to live there except the people who had nowhere else to live.

Snow hadn't accumulated in the city core, but out here there was a thin layer of white over everything. The odd assortment of temporary and semi-permanent buildings never looked better. The deeper snow near the hedgerow showed signs of rabbits and deer passing through. It made me wish I had taller boots with me.

Mort let Nelly out of the back and introduced her to me. She was a slightly shaggier, canine version of her partner, who looked like a human golden retriever. She gave me her paw and let me make a fuss of her for a couple of minutes. Then it was time for her to work.

"Crabbe says there are a couple of clearings in the hedgerow," said Mohr. "Collins grew up in Stinktown and knew the area well. As teens, they'd party in there until the Stinktowners found them and kicked them out."

"I need to give Nelly space," said Mort. "You need to give me space. Kate, Nelly's met you so you can stay with me. The rest of you hang back."

"Kate's injured," said Jake.

"That's okay. Nelly won't mind." Mort pulled a walking stick out of his HUV and handed it to me. "That'll help you keep your balance."

On the whole, despite the cold, wet and rough terrain, staying with Mort was probably the softer option. The Chief was angry at me. Jake was confusing me. And less of Mohr would probably be a good thing right now.

There was a clear area close enough to the road that I could see the black HUVs through the bare branches. Mort signalled me to stop while Nelly traversed the area, back and forth, sometimes stopping, but never lying down to indicate she found something. Periodically, Nelly would look back at Mort, Mort would look back at me and I'd look back at Jake following at a distance.

After a while the dull ache in my hand grew sharper. My painkillers were wearing off. On the upside, the effects of the opiates on my brain were wearing off too.

Crabbe said he witnessed Blake and Irene Collins get into a car with Therese Marten. Why? He didn't live near the Collins's at the time. What was he doing at the apartment complex?

If, as I deduced, Marten was the one under duress, would Collins have been able to force her into the car on his own? Maybe. Would he be able to do it without

Crabbe figuring out what was going on? Less likely. Would he have got help from Crabbe? More likely.

Nelly looked back at Mort. Mort looked back at me. I nodded. I don't know if he was looking for my permission to continue, but he had it.

However he may have aided Collins, Crabbe didn't go along for the drive. He didn't know what had happened to his friend. Irene probably knew and was burdened with that knowledge.

What did Koehne know? How did Koehne know Crabbe and Collins? Would they have gone to the same high school? How did the daughter of a prominent business man marry a guy from Stinktown? Mr. Koehne Sr. was a good tenant and always treated me with courtesy, but he was a snob. Had Irene been a rebel before her spirit was broken?

What was Koehne Jr. afraid of?

I stubbed my toe on something under the snow and silently swore a blue streak. How the hell did Collins persuade Marten to walk this far?

Nelly looked back Mort. Mort looked

back at me. I looked through bare branches to my right on a field, lightly sprinkled with snow, and dirt road, wide enough for a tractor.

Not long after, Nelly lay down. She'd found something. It was near a fallen tree that might have created an open space under its canopy when it was alive. Now it made a great bench.

23

I was cold, tired and in a world of pain but I would have handcuffed myself to a tree rather than leave now.

Nelly had done her job. She had found human remains. They could belong to someone unrelated to the case but, unless she was off her game, someone had been buried here. Mort placed a flag and Nelly sniffed around, finding nothing else. Mort took her aside and made a fuss of her, telling her what a good dog she was. I followed and made a fuss of her and discovered that if she hadn't found anything, it would have been my job to hide so she could find me.

"We can't let her get frustrated," said Mort. "Finding the body is her payoff in the game."

"But I'm not dead."

"That's okay. She's a search and rescue dog too."

Nelly and Mort stayed until the

IDENT team showed up with a scanner. That's what I was waiting for too. I'd seen them demonstrated, but never in the field. On uneven ground, it required two people in harnesses to manipulate the scanner while a certified technologist focussed and analysed the images. The tech also told the people holding the machine where to go and what to do when they got there.

Mort's nephew Ziggy came along to hoist the scanner even though he was a microbiologist and forensic pharmacologist. Mort offered to help, but their heights were too disparate. If Ziggy had been a dog, he would have been a Greyhound, extra-long.

The Chief was the closest match in height, so he donned the harness. The technologist, a woman I would have to buy drinks for some day, briefed the Chief on what she expected and what she'd do to him if he didn't pay attention.

The Chief nodded and tried not to look like he was having fun with the one of the regional forensic centre's most expensive toys.

As soon as everything was set up, Jake and Mohr sat on either side of me on the fallen tree. For a moment I thought they might start a tug of war, but then I realized they were trying to warm me up. It was a bit claustrophobic, but I didn't have time to worry about it.

"Quiet everyone. The scanner is calibrated and can be accessed with passkey 2BY49. That's Two. Bravo. Yankee. Four. Niner."

Those of us who could, pulled out our eCom's and logged on. Jake didn't have a police issue eCom, so he watched mine. Mort looked over my shoulder until Nelly got restless.

It was like watching an ultrasound with less movement. Even when we saw something, we couldn't be sure what it was. I wished I'd brought my tablet but I'm not sure it would have helped.

Then there was black shape.

"Hold," said the technologist. The shape resolved. It looked like the negative of a spine. "If you want a better idea of what you're looking at, switch to enhanced mode. It's at the top of the screen."

Mohr and I switched views. Real time, the scanner only showed the section it was focussed on. In enhanced mode, the program built a picture based on the collection of images.

"What are you seeing?" asked the Chief.

"It's a human skeleton," I said. "Judging by the pelvis, it looks male."

"That's my conclusion too," said the technologist. "You'll need a forensic anthropologist to view this for confirmation, but as long as you don't quote me, these remains are consistent with the subject you were looking for."

The Chief started barking orders. Mohr was designated the scene's gatekeeper. It was up to him to record who was on the scene, for how long and what reason.

His first task was to release Mort and Nelly so they could go home. Then he had to call in support to secure the scene. The soil sampler was given the job of getting a full IDENT team on site.

"Are you done, Chief?" asked the

technologist. "Because I'm not. There's more down there–at least two more sets of remains and what looks like a police badge.

24

"This is a police case now."

Jake and I were sitting at the Thorsen kitchen table again and the Chief had just stated the obvious. I tried counting to keep myself from saying something I'd regret later. Then I couldn't help myself.

"Seriously? A woman with multiple broken bones, a cat with a broken neck and a man whose skull looks like it was split with an axe lie in a single grave. Of course it's a police case, but it's also our case."

"That is an assumption based on circumstantial evidence only. Until the remains are unearthed and positively identified, we don't know if they are related or not. For now, I think Jacob should take you home."

My head hurt. My hand ached. And my godfather was getting on my nerves.

"I agree," said Jake.

For a moment I thought he was

agreeing with me. No such luck.

"There is no point jumping to conclusions when forensic evidence can give us answers."

The Chief nodded.

"Besides, we have a more urgent matter."

Curiosity got the better of my anger and I wondered, what urgent matter Jake was referring to?

"What urgent matter?" the Chief asked.

"I need your help with an intervention. Kate has been insisting on doing all the packing in Joe's apartment herself, even though she has to have it clear by the New Year so the ceiling can be replaced. Joe never got around to taking care of the water damage from last spring. I wasn't going to interfere, but she can't do it by herself especially with a bad hand."

I had been clenching eyes shut hoping this wasn't really happening. A huge paw I identified as godfather's hand covered mine. I opened my eyes.

"I had no idea, Katie girl. I should

have known."

Now I was going to cry. Why did Jake have to do this to me?

"I know you want to kill me right now," Jake said, laying a hand on my shoulder. "But I'm not trying to undermine your duty to your father. I'm just suggesting that you don't have to do it all at once. If we pack everything up and put it in storage, the work can be done and you can go through everything later, one box at a time."

"He's making good sense," said the Chief. "We can put a posse together between the holidays."

"You won't be too busy?" I asked.

"I'm never too busy for family." He looked as sheepish a man who looks like a Norse god can. "At least, I try not to be."

I looked over to Jake and gave him a wan smile. It was all I was up for.

The Chief gave my good hand a squeeze. Then he was all business.

"Take her home, Jacob. The girls have packed up both of your things. Don't worry about the bones. We're not likely to get them identified before January anyway."

"Agreed," said Jake. "And if Blake Collins' bones are there, you'll bring us in?"

"Of course."

I kept my mouth shut. Jake had just managed me and the Chief like a pro. I was impressed.

In the car, Jake asked me the million dollar question.

"Where is home tonight?"

It was about time I made up my mind. "Dad's place which, thanks to you, is going to be my place soon."

"Good choice. Will your ex be fine with it?"

"I think he's been waiting for me to come to that decision."

"He's a good friend."

I laughed. "Better friend than boyfriend, that's for sure."

For a few blocks I just watched the holiday lights go by. I hoped no cats died while we were occupied. Knowing where the bodies were buried wasn't as helpful as I hoped.

"I'd bet dollars to donuts that those remains belong to Detective Marten, Blake Collins and Irene's cat."

"I agree," said Jake. "Do you think Crabbe was there? I don't buy that he watched Marten force Blake and Irene into the car and just stood by."

"No. I don't think he went with them, but I think he was an accessory to kidnapping. I'd love to charge him with accessory to murder if only just to get him to come clean about that night. I've got a feeling Collins only planned to run off with his wife. Marten showed up at the wrong time."

"Assuming Collins killed Marten. Who killed Collins?"

"Who's left?"

Jake got me settled on the office couch before going home. It was comfortable and there was nothing in sight to tempt me to pack or clean instead of rest. He set me up with a couple of books, a mug of green tea and a bottle of over-the-counter analgesics.

"I'll be back in a couple of hours with dinner," he promised.

"There's still a cat killer on the loose."

"We'll strategize about that after dinner."

The books he brought were from my father's light reading collection. These included the Goddaughter novellas and a mystery anthology: "Behind Locked Doors." I chose the anthology. I wasn't sure I'd be awake long enough to read a novella.

I didn't make it through the first story.

Half an hour later, I woke up to a niggling thought that was almost lost in the noise of my eCom announcing an urgent call. It was Irene Cole.

"Detective Garrett, Blake is back. I saw him on the street."

"Have you called the police?"

"I can't," she said. There was a pause. "This has happened before. They don't believe me anymore."

"Are the doors and windows locked?"

"Yes."

"Are you alone in the house?"

She hesitated.

"My brother was here, but he left. It's just me here. It's just like before."

I took stock. One hand out of commission–my dominant hand, plus the all over achy feeling you get from pushing yourself too hard in the cold and damp. Nothing new. Jake had the company car and wasn't due back for almost an hour. I could take a cab or walk down the street to the community car depot or I could just call ERC and send a patrol car to the house.

"Detective Garrett?"

"I'll be right there."

25

I opted for a cab and messaged Jake to meet me at Irene's. Instead of struggling with a change of clothes, I borrowed Jake's hoodie again and hoped the cab was well-heated. I didn't think I could get my coat on by myself.

On the way over I set up my eCom for emergencies. Seconds later, I got a call from ERC.

"Garrett, I have you headed for East Hills. Are you taking another walk in the park? If you are, I want you to change your keyword."

"I'm going to a private home."

"Do they have pets?"

I counted to three. "Seriously?"

"No, that won't work. You Garretts use that word to death."

The cab stopped. The driver receipted me and drove away as soon as I was on the sidewalk. I took a moment to look around. No one was lurking within sight.

Irene's house was dark. Even the porch light was off. That was helpful. The one-way glass in the transom worked wasn't as effective when it was dark. With blue glow of the security system screen, I could make out two people moving in the hall.

I checked my eCom. Jake was a block or so away. Close enough.

I rung the bell and talked to the intercom.

"Ms. Cole, it's Detective Garrett."

I waited a few seconds and tried again.

"Irene, please. It's Kate Garrett. Please come to the door."

Finally I heard Irene's voice.

"I'm here. I have to unlock the door."

Deadbolts clicked and chains rattled. The door opened a crack.

"You can come in."

I opened the door enough to see most of the hall. Irene backed away. She was biting her lip and wringing her hands. Since I couldn't see the second person, I guessed he was behind the door. That put him on my bad side.

No problem. I kicked the door. There was an "oomph" sound and the door bounced back to reveal Paulo Crabbe.

I'd been hoping it was Mike Koehne.

I had my pistol aimed at him but Crabbe launched himself at me anyway. He was what my Grandmother Garrett called "bottle covey." He didn't have the sense to stay down. He was also damned lucky. My aim wasn't as good with my left hand. Instead of hitting centre mass, my shot went wide. The bullet hit his hip and he still kept coming, knocking me over.

"Crap!" I had to drop my pistol to grab Crabbe's arm. He was holding a tranquilizer dart. If it was loaded with cyanide, I might be joining my father in the family plot.

I needed both hands to keep the dart at arms distance. Crabbe could have tried harder but he preferred to use his free hand to punch me. My best hope was that he'd bleed out before he smartened up.

Belay that. My best hope was Jake who twisted the dart out of Crabbe's hand. He then kept twisting and pulling, to accompanying screams, until Crabbe was off me, hanging from a broken wrist and dislocated shoulder. That didn't stop Crabbe from screaming and flailing about.

I pulled myself up and pushed my Taser against his bad leg. Crabbe twitched and went as limp as a rag doll. Jake let him down easy and cuffed him. I would have been tempted to drop him on his head.

Irene kicked him. Then she threw her arms around me and started crying.

Mohr was the first official responder. He came in as Jake and I were trying to calm Irene. He directed the ambulance and police escort for Crabbe, called the Chief and sent a rookie out on a coffee run.

Jake and I got Irene settled in the living room. She allowed a paramedic to check my hand and tend my face. She accepted a sublingual anti-anxiety tab and followed the directions to count backwards from thirty while the tab dissolved under her tongue. The counting was almost as important as the medicine. It gave her mind something else to do besides panic.

It helped that the paramedic was a woman. Irene also accepted Jake as Joe's partner.

She stiffened when Mohr came in and started to freak when the Chief arrived. Her husband had been a big man. The Chief was a very big man.

"Irene, look at me," I said, using my good hand to turn her face away from the Chief-filled entrance. "Tell me what happened. Focus on me."

The Chief back out into the hall and leaned against the far wall. Irene started to breath normally again.

"Why was Paulo Crabbe here?" I asked.

"He wanted to know what happened to Blake. I thought he knew. I thought Mike told him."

She glanced toward the hall. No one was there. I could see Mohr sitting on the stairs with his tablet out. I guessed the Chief was nearby. From Irene's view point, we were alone.

"I thought I could keep it secret, but I needed Mike's help getting rid of Blake's car. I thought Mike would take my side. I'm his sister. He was angry that Blake was dead–even when I told him what Blake did to me."

"What happened to Therese Marten?"

Irene swallowed a couple of times.

"Mike was supposed to go to the apartment to feed Suzy. I wanted him to pack some things for me too. He kept forgetting. He told me he'd meet me at the apartment so I could pack my own things and he'd take Suzy home with him. He wasn't there. Blake was."

She laced and unlaced her fingers.

"Would you like some water, Irene?" Jake asked.

She nodded. As soon as he was out of the room, she continued, voice pitched at a whisper.

"I'm so sorry. He made me call Therese and tonight Paulo made me call you. I couldn't warn you."

"But you tried."

I don't know if Irene knew I knew Blake was dead, but saying she saw him was a giveaway. The long pauses after certain question. She was being fed lines by someone else, someone who didn't know that Irene had told me she hadn't seen Blake since he disappeared.

"Who was with you when I came to the door?"

She tipped her head to one side, like a curious bird. "How did you know?"

"I didn't at the time," I admitted.

"That was Mike. He was afraid I'd say something to you. I've wanted to say something for years."

Jake returned with a tall glass of water. She gulped about half of it down. She took a tissue out of her sleeve, delicately patted her mouth dry and smiled. "I feel better now."

26

December 23

I took the stairs two at a time to the fourth floor. For the first time in weeks, I felt energized. My hand still hurt. I still missed my father. I still wished I could hibernate between Christmas Eve and New Year's Day. But today was a good day.

I had just come from Irene Cole's preliminary hearing. She confessed to killing her husband after he beat Therese Marten to death in front of her. The last straw was when he strangled her cat. A psychiatrist spoke to the issue of spousal abuse and how the abused might stand up to their abuser when they attack someone else.

The forensic anthropologist who examined the scans testified that evidence supported Ms. Cole's statement but warned that a definitive report could not be made at this time.

Given the apparent perimortem

injuries suffered by Marten, Irene hitting her husband with the spade he brought along to bury the body seemed perfectly reasonable.

Her lawyer argued that it was self-defence, since Ms. Cole could have been the next victim.

Pending the complete retrieval of the skeletal remains and their thorough investigation to confirm cause of death, Irene Cole was being remanded to the mental health centre.

I opened the door to the lobby and saw Koehne sitting in one of the chairs we had for waiting clients.

"Good afternoon, Mr. Koehne."

Koehne handed me an envelope.

"This is thirty days' notice," he said. "According to our agreement, for the first six months, either party can give thirty days' notice to terminate the lease if the arrangement proves unsatisfactory."

"You're unsatisfied?"

"Due to family obligations, I find advisable to go back to working out of my home."

"Understandable," I said. "Funny I didn't see you at the hearing. Given your sister's statement, I'm surprised you weren't subpoenaed."

He tried too hard not to react.

I tapped him on the shoulder with the envelope.

"Between you and me, seek legal counsel. You may be charged with accessory to murder. I can think of another half dozen other charges you may face when Paulo Crabbe starts to talk. Your sister might even decide to sue you for coercing her not to come forward earlier."

I left him to go upstairs and gave the envelope a little wave.

"Thanks for this."

"I'll be home for Christmas. You can count on me…"

I listened to Jake sing from the stairs. He had a good voice. If he could harmonize, we could bill ourselves as the singing detectives.

"I'll be home for Christmas, if only in my dreams. I know you're there, Kate."

"Good. Now you can't complain if I sing in the office."

I headed for the kitchenette.

"Making cafe au lait?" Jake asked.

"Coffee nog," I said, holding up a bottle of the best commercially made egg nog in the province. "We're celebrating."

"The solving of the Cat-killer Caper?"

I laughed. "You tell me. How did the search of Crabbe's property go?"

"He had workshop in the basement with darts, lab equipment and the making for pipe bombs."

"Yikes!"

"It's clear he was the cat killer. They might even get him to confess in exchange for not charging him with urban terrorism. You did a good job solving that mystery."

I smiled and passed Jake his coffee nog. I liked us getting along, but I had to come clean. "I went in circles trying to tie it into the Collins case. The people were tied to one another, but the two cases were separate. The bits finally came together while I was sleeping.

"Crabbe might have loved his cats, but he was pretty cold-blooded otherwise. He wanted to punish cat owners that let their pets run loose. Where other people might have started a campaign, he made his statement with violence."

"He was a man with a mission."

"A sociopath with a mission," I said. "I'm just glad he tried to kill me."

Jake gave me an incredulous stare.

"I'm also glad he failed, thanks to you. But crimes against persons carry a lot more weight in sentencing than crimes against animals. But that's not why we're celebrating."

"Oh?"

I raised my mug of nog. "My tenant has given his notice. I should be sorry about the loss of income but mostly I am hugely relieved, especially since said tenant may be looking at jail time. So cheers!"

Jake stood to clink mugs with me but he seemed distracted. I didn't expect him to be dancing for joy, but his lack of response was raining on my parade.

"Is there something wrong?"

He shook his head and half sat on the end of my desk. "Before you rented the suite to Koehne, I was thinking of making you an offer on the space. I thought I could convert it to an apartment. When you offered me Joe's place, it didn't feel right. But I did get to thinking it would be nice to be closer to the office than I am now. What do you think?"

"Shit."

"You don't like the idea," he said, sounding hurt.

"No, I think it's brilliant. I wish I thought of it. The tax rebate for creating new residential space will cover a big chunk of the renovation costs, and I won't have an annoying deadbeat for a tenant." I grinned at him. "At least, you better not be an annoying deadbeat."

"I also had an idea about Christmas," he said. "Come home with me. My aunt and uncle would be happy to have you."

Yikes! Was he feeling sorry for me?

I thought about the sandwiches, threatening Koehne on my behalf, trying to keep me warm in the cold and a dozen other practical demonstrations of affection. Even the ruthless violence he showed getting Crabbe off me was a clue.

Some detective you are, Garrett.

"Thanks, Jake, but I can't. Mum and David made last minute plans for me to go skiing with them.

"I'm not crazy about skiing and I'm not sure I'll actually ski with this hand, but they want me there." I shrugged. "They think I need to get away."

"They're probably right." He shrugged. "Maybe next year."

He got up and headed back to his desk. For a moment he was under the mistletoe.

It was tempting. Very, very tempting.

Then the moment passed.

Maybe next year.

~

Excerpt from Deadly Legacy (Prequel to Deadly Season)

I was seven years old the first time my father me to work. Back then, detectives had their own desks and the locker room was segregated. As he gave me the tour, he described the bullpen when he was shown around by his mother. The grey steel desks were the same but back then, vacuum tube computer monitors and hard-wired keyboards took up most of the available surface area. The rest was covered in stacks of paper, personal items and coffee cups.

In turn, his mother painted another picture of a squad room, the one she'd visited as a child.

Desks were made of wood. No computers, at least none generally available to the detectives. Officers entered information in their Occurrence Books. Reports were produced on temperamental electric typewriters.

Policing ran in the family.

Now *Occurrence Book* was the name of

the police-specific software that we used to record information on our eComs.

Workstations with composite oak-like desks were equipped with flip-up flat-screen monitors, keyboards and docking ports so detectives could plug in, upload or download files and generate reports which could be read on other screens.

The stations were like hotel rooms. Officers moved in for as long as they needed the space, spreading their personal property out — or not — according their personality.

Detectives carried their 'offices' with them in a briefcase, backpack, or in some cases their pockets.

One thing that hadn't changed was the coffee cups. There were *always* coffee cups, some half-filled with five-day-old sludge, some clean. 'World's Best Mom' or 'Dad' or 'Fisherman' could be found among the collection, along with the inevitable 'Detectives do it with cuffs.'

I found my *Much Ado* cast mug in the drying rack of the kitchenette. I dialled up a dark roast and set it under the coffee machine to fill.

Soon, I was warming my chilled

hands on the hot ceramic. I staked out a desk and plugged in my eCom. While it went through its automatic virus check and login, I headed toward the locker room and dry clothes.

In my father's day the room was a labyrinth of grey lacquered lockers and matching benches.

Now the locker room was more like a communal living room, complete with family photos and kids' art. There were comfy chairs and a couch at one end, and an ironing board, hair dryers and vanity mirrors at the other.

The lockers were generously sized for multiple changes of clothes and a full range of toiletries. Being a modern police officer meant always going out looking professional, even if you came back looking like something the cat dragged in.

"If you give it to me now, I can save the suit. The shoes are toast."

I turned and passed the water-stained wool jacket into the outstretched hands of Detective Vincent Valerio, a pleasant-looking man of uncertain years and somewhat academic demeanor.

He reminded me of Mr. Chips, without the cap, gown and English accent. Vince was one of a handful of people still in the department who had known my father when he was a police detective, before a gunshot wound and resulting complications forced him into medical retirement.

He gave me the bring-it-on hand gesture. "Pants, too. You can launder your own blouse, I imagine."

"You don't have to, Vince," I said, reaching for the jacket. "I thought you were kidding."

He swung the garment out of reach. "You know I don't kid about clothes. Get out of those damp things and into something warm."

He bestowed a disarming grin. It transformed his face at once from mildly attractive to rather handsome.

"Everyone knows rookies get all the worst jobs, but that suit did nothing to deserve such bad treatment. Has no one told you about raincoats?"

I let him have the suit.

Stripping off the rest of my wet clothes, I dumped them into the laundry bag in my locker and selected a warm sweater and linen pants from the clothes I kept at work.

Then I fluffed my short chestnut hair and applied fresh lipstick. It was the only makeup I wore off stage. Without it, my pale lips disappeared on my pale face.

Mercy waited by my desk. Except for a little mud spattered on her boots, her black hair, lace-trimmed t-shirt and leather pants were immaculate. The effect was only slightly spoiled by the fact Mercy looked nervous.

"Thorsen wants to see you."

"What did I do this time?"

Mercy pursed her lips and nodded toward the docking port. "Take everything. I'll generate the reports. I'll be around if you want to talk."

I disengaged my eCom and picked up my mug. It was probably *not* a good idea to walk in to see the Chief of Detectives with a cup of coffee in hand, but the brew had just reached the perfect temperature for drinking.

I compromised by taking an extra minute to gulp down half the cup, then poured the remainder in the sink. Wiping a dribble of coffee off my chin I paused outside the only enclosed office in the suite, took a deep breath, and then knocked.

The chief opened the door and ushered me in. This didn't bode well. His usual response was bellowing, "Come in."

Usually, I felt like a shrimp in the presence of my boss. I was particularly short and there was nothing wispy or fragile about me, but Chief Igor Thorsen was a giant of a man. He looked like an over-sized Viking warrior with long red-blonde hair, a full beard and the hint of a Norwegian accent. "Large as life and twice as ugly," my father would joke. Except right now. The behemoth seemed deflated.

"What's wrong, Chief?"

"Kathleen...it's your father."

And then I knew. The knowledge closed in on me, shutting down my ability to react, to speak, to take a breath. It wasn't just the Chief who had shrunk. The whole world had suddenly grown smaller.

Continued in Deadly Legacy (Second Edition)

About the Author

Alison Bruce has an honors degree in history and philosophy, which has nothing to do with any regular job she's held since. A liberal arts education did prepare her to be a writer, however. She penned her first novel during lectures while pretending to take notes.

Her books combine clever mysteries, well-researched backgrounds and a touch of romance. Her protagonists are marked by their strength of character, sense of humor and the ability to adapt (sooner or later) to new situations. Four of her novels have been finalists for genre awards.

www.deadlypress.com

Printed in Great Britain
by Amazon

84995452R00114